Christmas '92.

BREAKING
The CIRCLE

To Clare,
    from Santa.

*For Sinéad, a critical reader
and for Brian*

About the author: Desmond Kelly is originally from Glasnevin in Dublin and he now lives in Drumcondra. He is a secondary school teacher in Ballymun and has been published previously in *The Sunday Tribune*. This is his first novel.

BREAKING The CIRCLE

Desmond Kelly

ACE
FICTION

WOLFHOUND

First published 1992 by
WOLFHOUND PRESS
68 Mountjoy Square
Dublin 1

Wolfhound Press receives financial assistance from The Arts Council/
An Chomhairle Ealaíon, Dublin, Ireland.

British Library Cataloguing in Publication Data
    A catalogue record for this book is available from
    the British Library

    ISBN 0-86327-348-3

This book is fiction. All characters, incidents and names have no
connection with any persons living or dead. Any apparent resem-
blance is purely coincidental.

Cover design: Fiona Lynch
Typesetting: Wolfhound Press
Printed in Great Britain by Cox & Wyman Ltd., Reading, Berks.

1

'Shit,' said Sorcha, and sat up suddenly. She immediately felt dizzy. It was not the sort of dizziness that might lead to her fainting but the nearly pleasant kind where everything, the blue sky, the view over the city and the sweep of curving coastline, the glittering sea and the islands, were all slightly displaced, all swam out of focus. She remained still, knowing that things would settle back to normal after a few moments.

She loved it on the mountain. It was her favourite walk, all the way up from Marley Park, through the woods, along the winding path with glimpses of the view until, at the top she felt, always, elated. The city, which was so noisy and busy and exciting when she was in it was, from the mountain, a toy town spread helplessly below. She felt she could do anything with it, move bits here or there as she had a whim to. The huge TV mast behind her helped her fantasy along. The signals were beamed up to the mountain from the studios down below and from there they were broadcast over the whole city. She was always enchanted by these silent, unseen waves bringing the pictures into all those houses. They were clever to site the masts here where nothing blocked their access to the city. She felt that it was her own mental energy radiating to each house, to each little box in each little corner, bringing fun, mystery, excitement, news. Sometimes she even felt that she could patch into the signals and send her own messages. She enjoyed thinking of the shock a family might get if their favourite chat show was interrupted.

She had a special boring family that she used for imagining scenes like this. There was a mother who never did anything except shop and cook and wash and, naturally, complain. There was a father who worked in an insurance company, wore a suit and polished shoes, who went to work every day and came home for his dinner at six, watched television until eleven and then went to bed. At weekends he washed his company car and played golf with his clients. He only saw the children on Sundays and on holidays. There were two children. Alice, the eldest was so good you wanted to hit her. She wore clothes that were always out of fashion. She always did what she was told and was very responsible. She helped her mother and did her homework and had no interest in boys. She watched a lot of television and her father called her his little peach. She was fifteen. Simon was ten and he was a brat. He stole Alice's money and lied to his parents. He often used bad language but was never caught by his parents or teachers. He was always top of his class and everyone (except Alice) loved him.

These were the Smiths. Sorcha had invented them and liked to use them when she was particularly displeased with her life, or when she was feeling very annoyed with, or superior to, most people in the world.

There beside the transmitters she imagined all the Smiths watching a really boring programme (cartoons or an old black and white film) and her inner thoughts, some of the very worst ones, the ones she told nobody about, flashing onto their screen. 'My goodness, what on earth is that?' shouts Mrs Smith in dismay. Mr Smith stands up. He is wearing his cardigan because it's a holiday. 'How can they show this ... this ... this ...,' splutters Mr Smith, at a loss for words, waving his hands in the air. 'I pay my licence fee,' he finally gets out, 'I'll not have this. I've a good mind to complain.' Alice goes pale. She is so used to nice thoughts that she can't even understand what is on the screen. 'Oh ...,' she says weakly. Simon starts to giggle and stares at the TV with great interest, the first time he has shown enthusiasm all afternoon. Mr Smith blusters around looking for the remote control, switches the channel to sport, and sits down. He says again, 'I've a good mind to complain.' Mrs Smith echoes him, 'Licence fee,' she says.

Sorcha had been lying on the ground, offending the Smiths, looking at the brilliant sky when she remembered that she had to be home by four. It was two o'clock and even the walk to the bus alone would take at least an hour and a half. She would never make it.

'What's wrong?' asked Paul from beside her. 'Nothing,' she said and waited for her head to stop revolving. She and Paul had come to Three Rock Mountain a few times before. Sometimes the others jeered them, said they were going with each other - which didn't always seem like such a bad idea to Sorcha, but most of the time she was happier that they were friends. She liked being able to talk to him without worrying too much about what was going to happen next.

She turned to look at Paul, once the world had settled down. He was still lying there and she wondered had he been going to kiss her. She found herself wondering that more often lately. It felt as though he wanted to. She tried to imagine what it would be like to kiss Paul. She had kissed boys before, at parties, or in the park, but never very seriously. Never out like this, on their own, with no one about. That would be different. She thought she might like it. It'd be nice if she could ask him what he'd like, but that would be too personal.

'We'll have to hurry,' she said, 'look at the time.' She stood up and turned, gripping his wrist and leaning back to pull him up. He rose easily and he was standing right in front of her. They looked at each other for a moment and at the same time they leaned forward and their lips touched. His felt soft and cold. Their heads moved a little to the side. They were still gripping each other's wrists. Sorcha liked the feel of his lips but began to get embarrassed. He was putting his arm around her. She turned, standing close to him, and they looked for a moment at the city.

It was early in the New Year, almost the end of the Christmas holidays but the weather was beautifully warm and sunny. The sea sparkled. The sky was perfectly blue. The only flaw was the haze of smog over the city. They could see clearly where it began, at the shoreline. It was as if her dizziness was a permanent feature over Dublin, Sorcha thought.

'Let's go,' said Paul and they headed off down the stony path. Sorcha set the pace and they really hurried for the first while. She half ran and half walked. Paul trailed behind her and then every few minutes ran a few steps to catch up. After a while he started to get annoyed.

'What's the rush?' he asked, panting a little.

'I've to babysit for the Smiths. They're going out with Mom and Dad to dinner. I said I'd be home by four.' Sorcha did not like her parents' friends. She had modelled her imaginary family on them.

'Who're the Smiths?' Paul asked. He liked to know what was going on.

'Oh, they're not really the Smiths. I just think of them like that. They're family friends. Yucky old bores. She knits. Imagine that. The baby's nice though. And I'll get a fiver.'

'Does that mean a pressie for me?' asked Paul with mock hope in his voice.

'Yeh, I'll get Mrs Bore to knit you a woolly scarf for your neck.'

They had slowed down while they were talking and Sorcha watched the sun flashing as they passed the trees.

'What sort of trees are those?' she asked.

'I don't know, firs or something. Christmas trees,' Paul told her.

'I bet there's reindeer around here, in the woods,' said Sorcha.

'I'll bet,' said Paul, 'and I heard that Santa Claus has his house near the transmitter.' He looked behind him at the metal latticed towers which rose up over the trees. They were visible from all over, like the power station chimneys in Ringsend.

'It's true,' said Sorcha, joining in the game. 'You should see this place on Christmas Eve. It's a hive of activity with elves and bags and reindeer heading out to the four corners of the globe.' At the last words she jumped onto a small rock and raised her voice and moved her arm stiffly in front of her to take in everything, in imitation of the street preachers she had seen once in London. Paul ran over and pushed her off. He leapt into her place.

'They will travel through the night, through thick and thin, hauling behind them their gifts of toys, of magic, of true love and friendship. They will fight hardship and evil, betrayal and ugliness mischievousness and school exams...'

'And my dad, if we don't hurry,' Sorcha interrupted him, taking his hand and rushing off down the path.

By the time they got on the bus it was a quarter to four. Sorcha knew that in the heavy afternoon traffic she would be lucky to get home by half past. They ran up the stairs together and flopped into the front seat. 'Ladies and Gentlemen of the bus,' began Sorcha, standing up and turning to face the other passengers. Paul burst out laughing and grabbed her, pulling her down. 'Shut up, you donkey. You'll ruin me dead with embarrassment.'

When the bus reached her stop, Sorcha arranged her face so that she would look suitably apologetic for her parents. It was nearly a quarter to five and it had got very cold since darkness had fallen but she felt warm inside, and thought of Paul.

2

A week later school had started. It was Saturday and the gang were going ice-skating.

'How do they keep all that water frozen?' asked Molly. She was fourteen and not the brightest member of the gang.

'Look,' said Jeff, always willing to have a laugh at someone's expense. 'How do you make ice at home?'

'Put it in the fridge,' said Molly, looking at him expectantly.

Sorcha muttered to Paul, 'Look at her wide eyes. She'll believe anything he tells her.' Paul smiled.

'No, Molly', said Jeff in his mock-serious voice, 'you put water in the fridge and it becomes ice, below zero degrees Celsius.'

'That's right,' said Molly, 'we did that at school.'

'Now you see,' said Jeff and turned away. He looked up the road, 'Will that bus ever come?' he asked the whole group.

Molly looked confused. She had been waiting for more.

Paul joined in. 'Don't tell me you still don't get it?' he asked her.

'Of course I do', said Molly, embarrassed at not under-standing.

'Oh, my God,' said Sorcha, and laughed when she caught Paul's eye. Jeff was grinning like a cat.

'Here's the bus,' shouted Sonny, almost jumping up and down with excitement. He was twelve and they let him come along only because his mother and Sorcha's were good friends. Her mother always asked her to take him and she reluctantly agreed. None of the others paid much attention to him and Sorcha felt she had to talk to him now and again, as he was her responsibility.

Sorcha was best on the ice. She knew that. Her father had brought her often when she was smaller. Some of the others were good, but not in her class at all. Paul was athletic and was getting the hang of it quickly. She loved the feel of gliding, when she got into her stride. The pressure of her weight, first on one leg, one skate, pushing her forward and out to the side, her body leaning into it; then, just before she passed the point where her balance would shift and she would tip over it was a swing of the weight onto the other leg, her hips adjusting, the right skate coming off the ice, the knee bent, leaning into it again, the others whizzing by, faster, faster, the lights, the thrumming of the music, sweating, skating until finally, panting and worn out she would whirl into the partition and lean there, gasping and exhilarated, laughing and laughing.

Now she watched Paul, knowing he had been watching her, unable to keep up. He was leaning forward, his hands behind his back, building up speed. Yes, he's getting good, she thought. A bit too flashy, though. None of the others are up to him at all. Except me. He shot past Frank on the turn, almost tipping him over. Frank was all right, but he was very serious, thought Sorcha. He was a wizard at school. A bit of a bore, though. He really took everything too seriously for a fifteen-year-old.

She noticed that Frank was annoyed with Paul. He called something after him but it was lost in the shouting and music. Paul was coming right down the centre of the rink, heading straight for her. He was going too fast and having slight problems with his balance. Sonny was moving across the ice, half walking, half skating. Paul was pushing hard into his left side when he saw Sonny. He had no time to think. He drew up his right leg, put both his skates together and did his best to keep to the left, trying to cross Sonny's path in front of him. He almost made it. Had he been just a little more in control he would have. As it was his arms were flailing and his outstretched right one caught

Sonny on the shoulder. Sonny jerked against the force of the blow and his skates shot out from under him. Paul tried to turn to see if Sonny had survived but he was going too fast and his skates were too close together. He slipped, landed on his hip and continued to slide until he hit the barrier just beside Sorcha.

Sorcha thought she had heard Sonny's head hit the ice. He had come down hard enough and was lying quite still. Two of the supervisors arrived beside him just as she did. They helped him to the side of the rink and took off his skates. The supervisors looked concerned and one of them got Sonny a drink of water. Sorcha thought he looked confused and in shock.

Gradually the whole group arrived. Sonny looked up at them now and then but said nothing. Sorcha desperately tried to remember what she had heard about concussion.

'You OK Sonny?' asked Paul, limping to his side. Sonny said nothing.

Molly crouched beside Sonny, turned and almost shouted, 'Fat lot of good it is asking, at this stage. It's all your fault - showing off.' She turned back to Sonny and put her hand on his forehead.

Frank joined in, 'Yes, Paul, you nearly knocked me over as well. Accidents don't just happen, you know. You should have been a lot more careful.'

'He's probably got concussion,' said Molly, 'We'll have to explain to his parents. I'm not going to cover up for you, Paul.'

Sorcha wasn't paying much attention to all this. She was worried about Sonny, pale and quiet in the middle of them all. The supervisors were not much help. They were only a few years older than the rest of them and not very well trained.

'There'll be no hidden scandals here,' said Jeff, getting at Molly because of her comment on not covering up for Paul.

'Shut up, all of you,' said Pam. 'This is no joke, Jeff. It was an accident. I saw it. Sonny came right across Paul's path. He couldn't avoid him.'

'What's this, you defending Paul? Fancy him, d'you, Pam?' snapped Molly angrily. 'We all saw that it was his fault, showing off.' Pam was Sorcha's best friend: they'd known each other since they were small.

'How're you feeling, Sonny?' Sorcha asked, crouching in front of him.

'I'm OK now,' he said. 'My head's sore, though.'

Sorcha could see a bruise starting up on his temple. 'I think you'll live to skate again,' she said. Sonny smiled. Sorcha looked up and caught Paul's eye. 'He's all right,' she said. She glanced around at the others and stood up so that she was beside Paul. 'The masses are revolting,' she muttered.

They decided to leave and get a hamburger on the way home. They were going to buy one between them for Sonny, to compensate for his injury, they told him.

'To shut him up so he won't squeal,' Jeff announced to anyone who wanted to listen.

On the way to the take-away Simone, Jeff's sister, came up to Paul and linked his arm. 'It must have been awful for you, Paul,' she cooed. 'Such a fright you must have got - and that old Molly and Frank attacking you. You were so brave.'

Sorcha was walking beside Paul and could see that he was laughing at Simone. He didn't unlink her arm though.

'Yes, Simone, it was terrible. No one even notices my injury.' Paul limped a little as he looked straight into her eyes and she sighed.

Sorcha was thinking that Simone was harmless. She never stopped reading romantic magazines and was boy crazy. She was very keen to go with Paul, but Sorcha knew that he was above all her nonsense.

'Oh, yes, Paulsey-Walsey! He got a tewibble fwight, he did too,' said Sorcha, in her most honey sweet, and she hoped, sickening imitation of Simone.

Paul burst out laughing and turned to Simone, releasing his arm from hers. 'I'm OK, Sim, honest I am.'

As they got on the bus Smiley-Joe exclaimed, 'Wasn't that a perfect day out.' He was thirteen and a half and always in a good mood.

3

The next afternoon was one of those winter Sundays when the sky is overcast and it's freezing cold and nobody has anywhere to go. The clouds look as if they might bring snow and there is always the hope of school closing if it turns out to be very heavy. That was what the gang talked about for a while, standing outside Pam's house. They all wore heavy coats or anoraks and scarves and gloves. Hands shoved deep in their pockets, they jumped from foot to foot. It was only half two and already it was getting dark.

'It's hard to believe that the winter solstice has passed and that spring is on the way,' said Paul.

'What's the winter solstice?' piped up Molly, predictably.

Paul was about to start making fun of Molly but Sorcha suddenly felt sorry for her and suggested that they go for a walk to warm up. She pushed her arm through Paul's as they walked along and snuggled up against him. 'Keep me warm,' she said.

'I think Sonny's OK' he said after a while.

'Yeh, he's fine.' Sonny was half walking, half skipping beside Smiley-Joe and Molly, who were in front. The others were paying him more attention than usual because of the accident and the dark bruise on his head, and he was enjoying himself.

'I got a fright for a minute,' said Paul to Sorcha.

'I'd say you did,' she said and wondered what he wanted. Was he looking for sympathy? If he was, she wasn't going to give it to him. The whole thing had been his fault: trying to do things he wasn't able for. Simone could give him sympathy, if that was what he wanted. She kept her thoughts to herself: it would be too difficult and personal to talk about. Sorcha often felt she'd like to be able to talk to him about these things but it was hard with boys. Everything always seemed to be charged when you were talking to a boy. She supposed it was because there was always the chance that you'd start going with each other. She remembered kissing Paul the previous weekend and decided to try it again soon. She could talk to Pam about the personal stuff.

They came on to Griffith Avenue, wide and lined with bare winter trees. There was a vacant house on the avenue. The last family had moved out nearly two years before and no one had been living there since. The grass had been cut a few times but the place was developing a run down, tatty appearance. The more unkempt it became the more interested the gang was in it. Stories had been told about unusual happenings there. At first it was strange sightings. Some of the local children swore that they had heard cries from inside and even seen a woman at one of the upstairs windows. The younger ones would dare each other to run into the garden and once they all scared themselves so much that some of their parents met and banned them from going near the place. They contacted the Corporation about it but it seemed someone owned the house so they could do nothing about it. After that a window got broken and was not repaired.

Sorcha and her gang were, naturally, sceptical of these stories. Yet it was very hard to ignore them completely. This was probably why they joked about the house whenever they were near it. As they approached, Sorcha wondered idly how near they would get before Jeff remembered some tall story about the place. At some point they had begun to talk of it as a free house, as if they could have parties there. Sorcha had mixed feelings about that. It was exciting, sort of thrilling, thinking of what they might do. Yet in a funny way she was glad that it was only talk. At any rate, the ghosts provided a good excuse for keeping away.

One night the previous summer, Sorcha, Paul, Pam and Jeff had been passing when Jeff suggested they go into Miley's Place, as it was called, though nobody seemed to know why. They had gone around the back, making sure not to be noticed. The grass was knee high and Sorcha imagined scurrying animals as they came into the garden, their voices automatically dropping to whispers.

'Oh no, I stepped in poo,' said Jeff. He lifted his foot to examine it. 'I think it's human,' he said. 'Imagine what must have been going on here before we came.' He was about to launch into one of his extended vulgar stories when Sorcha said, 'Shut up, Jeff,' and they all turned their attention to the house. The dining room window was slightly open. The catch had been broken. Pam lifted the window and one by one they climbed in. Sorcha imagined that the only reason she couldn't hear the others' hearts was because her own was too loud. She wondered briefly what Alice Smith would do if she were here. Faint probably.

A fire had been lit in the grate. Pam examined the remains and decided it was not a family fire. It looked as if it had been lit with waste rather than with coal or turf. There were empty beer cans on the floor and in the fireplace, and little patches of cigarette butts here and there around the room.

'I wonder was it drugs?' said Paul.

'Yeh,' said Jeff, 'I think they were burning the furniture.' He had gone into the kitchen and reported that the doors had been torn off some of the presses. There were some wood chips scattered where they had been broken up.

'We'd better get out of here,' said Pam, uneasily.

'I hear a noise,' said Jeff, pausing in mid-step. He put his finger to his pursed lips and said, 'Sshh.'

They all waited, barely breathing. 'Boo! You gobshites,' he shouted. They all laughed, except Pam. 'We're going,' she said, sounding a bit shaky.

'Are you OK?' Paul asked her, and put his arm around her for a moment.

Over the winter their attitude had changed. The idea of using the place themselves for parties like the one that had caused the mess had been brought up. Winter was too cold for spending much time in an unheated, unlit house so nothing had actually come of it yet.

'Look at your man,' Smiley-Joe was saying as they walked along Griffith Avenue.

'He's weird,' said Molly, pulling a face.

'He's got a nice face. He's interesting,' said Simone, her dreamy look settling on her. Sorcha noticed that when Simone switched into her 'man mode' it was not just her face that changed but her whole body, the way she walked, the way she carried herself.

The object of their attention was a man walking towards them. He was tall and very, very thin. His blond hair was long and straggly, falling in front of his eyes. He jerked his head and the hair flicked backwards. He was carrying a small rucksack over one shoulder, and enormous woollen socks billowed out of the tops of his hiking boots, like smoke from the chimneys of a fiercely burning fire. He seemed to be very intense and was certainly paying no attention to them. Just before he reached them Jeff began, 'As I was saying, the hippie movement began in California in the 1960s. Many of these hippies, drop-outs from normal society, wore their hair long, carried their belongings in haversacks and wore very funny socks.'

'It was also well known,' Paul joined in, 'that they formed a separate culture, or sub-culture, based on drugs and ...' Sorcha was enjoying the banter but began to feel embarrassed for the man who was now close enough for her to see that he was probably not more than nineteen or so - not really a man, as she had thought at first. As it turned out, her concern was unnecessary because he went into Miley's Place before he reached them. He simply walked up the garden path and opened the hall door with a key. Everyone gaped to see what could be spotted inside the house.

'I don't believe it!' said Jeff.

'He must live in there,' said Pam.

'How could he?' asked Molly.

'Yeah,' said Simone, and returned to normal. It's as if she's gone off duty, thought Sorcha.

'Hey, I know,' said Smiley-Joe, 'I heard my mam talking. There's a new family moved in around here. My mam says they're a bit odd all right, into growing things, "self something or other", she said. I didn't know that it was Miley's Place though. Wait till I tell her.' He was delighted.

'Self what?' asked Pam.

'Self study or something. It means looking after yourself, keeping pigs and things.'

'Self sufficiency,' said Paul. 'Not being dependent on shops or factories for food and clothes and so on. Usually, though, you do it in the country, with a bit of land. It's probably only gossip.'

'It does look as if the socks were homemade,' laughed Sorcha.

They noticed that the window in the front had been replaced. Someone had done some work on the front garden as well, cutting the grass and digging up the old overgrown flowerbed.

'My goodness, Dear, what is this place coming to. Hippies in the houses. What next?' said Mrs Smith to her husband. 'Hippies, is it? I've a good mind to complain to the Corporation. Yes, I have. I pay my taxes,' said Mr Smith. 'Oh Daddy, do, they're dirty and smelly. There's poo in their garden. It's *horrible*,' said Alice, self-righteously. 'Poo. Oh, my goodness, how awful,' said Mr and Mrs Smith together. Simon smiled secretly and decided to pay a visit that very day.

Sorcha smiled at the thought as they headed for home.

4

'That's it, Sorcha. You either agree to it or you don't go.'

Sorcha didn't know whether to storm out of the room and slam the door good and hard behind her or to stay and argue her case yet again. She felt like slamming the door. Her anger was boiling inside her, wanting to shoot right out. Yet her practical side told her that if she did explode she'd lose this battle.

She wanted to go to a disco with Paul. It seemed simple enough to her. She was fifteen and a half, not a kid. The disco was fairly local and there were no fights, no gangs, no drink. She'd be going with Paul, staying with him while they were there and coming home with him. She'd be home by half eleven. No problem. Yet her father wanted to collect her afterwards. He had wanted to deliver her as well but had conceded on that one. Sorcha felt like going upstairs and trying on her Confirmation dress - anyone would think she was ten years old, the way he was going on.

She decided to do nothing for the moment. Conor might help when he came in, if he came in. Her brother was studying science at UCD and might as well be living there as at home. He went out in the morning and often only came home in time for bed. Sorcha was pretty sure that most of the time it was anything but study that kept him there. She didn't see that much of him these days but whenever he did talk about college life it sounded good

- much more relaxed than school. At least they treated you like an adult.

Sorcha sat down and turned on the TV. Her father stormed upstairs to change. The box flickered bluely to life. The sky outside was perfectly blue, except for one small cloud. The presenter said, 'Three Rock Mountain,' finishing off a news item and moved to the next topic. Sorcha continued to look at the screen but her mind returned to the day back in January, a day like this one, when she and Paul had first kissed. She did not want a row. She wanted to go to the disco and have some fun and enjoy the walk home. She wasn't going to do anything wrong. She was telling them exactly what she was doing. Would they ever let her grow up? Her exasperated question, often asked either to herself or aloud, in neither case was ever answered properly.

The hall door opened and Nuala, Sorcha's mother came in carrying her briefcase. 'Hi, Mom,' said Sorcha, deciding to try the cheerful approach. 'Hi, Sorcha, how're things?' called her mother and came over and kissed her. Sorcha asked her about her day and she began to tell her about a meeting of directors and how they were planning some new scheme or other. She worked in a bank and seemed to be always involved in huge decisions. She often had to travel to meetings. Sorcha supposed it was interesting, in a sort of a way. Her father worked in a department store in town. He was in charge of the men's department. He found it very boring and was always talking of doing something else. He worried a lot about money although Sorcha knew that between her mother and father they earned a good deal of it.

Her parents actually liked Paul and they quite approved of her going out with him. Her mother, though, had recently suggested that she was very young and shouldn't get too committed to any one boy. This annoyed Sorcha. She imagined that her parents had lost all their passion, if they could talk of planning being in love. She had been going with Paul for only two months, after all, since the middle of February. Sometimes that seemed an awfully long time, though she knew it wasn't really.

Her mother took off her jacket and went out to the kitchen and took mince meat from the fridge. Sorcha followed her and handed her her apron.

'What are we having?' she asked.

'Spaghetti. Will you set the table please?'

'Oh, OK,' said Sorcha. Recently she had gone right off spaghetti. She could only think of worms, slimy and tangled, slithering down her throat. She wondered whether there was something wrong with her. She had always liked spaghetti before, had thought of it as food.

'Mam.'

'Yes.' Her mother was concentrating on chopping an onion.

'Dad is insisting that he picks me up after the disco.'

'What's wrong with that?'

'It's so embarrassing. Everyone will think I'm a baby.'

'Come on, since when do you care what everyone thinks?'

'I'm not a kid. Nothing's going to happen me.'

'What do you want to do? Have a nice little session with Paul on the way home?' Her mother was teasing her.

'Ah, Mam, that's not it... of course I just might let him kiss me,' Sorcha said, joining in with her mother's playfulness.

'Oh, you might, might you? And what else might you do?' said Nuala, her tone jokey, still gently teasing.

'Well, you know, if it's cold I just might snuggle up for warmth, you know, beside a wall.'

'Well then, Eoin can solve that problem. He'll collect you in the car and you'll both be perfectly warm.' Nuala was serious, Sorcha knew, even though she was still making a joke of it.

Sorcha slammed down a plate on the table. 'Mother. I'm not a baby. I have to have some fun.'

'Sorcha, you're not an adult either. We're still responsible for you. When I was your age I wouldn't have been allowed near a dance on my own.'

'I won't be on my own, I'll be with Paul.' Sorcha was shouting now. Her father came into the room.

'I hope you're not at this again, Sorcha. I've told you what we've decided. No more about it, now.'

He began to get out some saucepans and asked Nuala how her day had gone. She started to tell him about her meeting. Sorcha looked at them standing there and decided that she had used them, not their friends, as her model for the Smiths. She was really angry. She liked her parents most of the time but they really treated her like a baby. Paul would be raging if they had to come home in the car. Everyone would be jeering. She supposed that some of the others would be collected too, but only those who lived far away, or who had rotten parents. It was OK in their day, they expected to be treated like kids, but this is different. She clattered the rest of the things on the table.

'Take it easy now,' said her father, 'no need to be bold.'

'Bold,' Sorcha exploded. 'Bold! You really do think I'm a baby.' She was so annoyed that she could feel the tears coming. She didn't want to cry in front of them so she ran out of the kitchen and pulled the door behind her. She hadn't intended to slam it so hard. She was only half way up the stairs when she heard the roar.

'Come back here.'

Sorcha waited as long as possible, to regain control of herself and to make him as angry as she could. Then she came slowly back to the kitchen. They were chatting as if nothing had happened. That was their trick to make her angry.

'You'd better change your attitude and apologise if you want to go at all.' It was her mother who spoke. There was no chance of them not putting up a united front. She hoped that Conor would arrive. He might rescue her. In her mind she said, I hate you Mr Smith. I hate you Mrs Smith. Out loud she said nothing.

'Well,' said her father waiting.

'Sorry,' she muttered, after a moment.

'For what?' demanded her mother. Give me a break Mrs Smith, Sorcha pleaded silently.

'For being rude, for disagreeing, for everything,' she said aloud, feeling sorry for herself by then.

'OK. Let's forget it,' said her father.

5

The one good thing about her father was that when he said to forget a row, he meant it. Her parents chatted through dinner as though nothing had happened. Sorcha didn't feel like talking and only joined in now and again so as not to draw attention to herself and make the situation worse. Conor didn't arrive and so she had to go through the whole meal with no distractions. Her parents rarely allowed the radio on during dinner, saying it ruined conversation. Sorcha would have been quite happy to have conversation ruined that day.

She decided to do her homework after dinner. It was one way to pass the time when she was so fed up and it would be out of the way and leave her time for anything interesting that might happen over the weekend. Maybe the car would break down and he wouldn't be able to collect her. It had been causing trouble recently so it was a possibility. She couldn't concentrate on her homework so she made a list of the disadvantages of the motor car. It might be useful if there was ever a debate on the topic in school and it suited her mood perfectly. Once she got going the ideas flowed along, a little to her surprise. She started with its interference with people's exercise. She went on to environmental issues. She had never really thought of the car in this way before. She imagined what the countryside was like before the roads had been built, what the cities would be like if there was only public transport. She thought of the air, of how a good deal of the smog was caused by exhaust fumes. That day in Three Rock had been warm with few enough fires and mainly smokeless fuel being burnt in them, yet she remembered looking across to Dublin Bay, and the haze of smog stretching to the shoreline. She was thinking of the social aspects of people's lives being improved if they walked to places together when she remembered that one of the titles for her weekend English essay was 'Is the motor car the curse or blessing of the twentieth century?' and realised with a start that she had it half planned. She got out her copy and began to write, forgetting all her earlier annoyance as she became absorbed.

'Swotting?'

Sorcha did not respond at first, because she did not hear anything.

'I said, are you swotting?' asked Paul. She looked up at him and smiled, although she felt a little irritated with him for interrupting her. He didn't usually call on Fridays.

Paul had arrived a little while before and had been talking to Eoin and Nuala in the other room. They had been watching TV and turned it off when he came in. Paul had often noticed they did that: very few adults bothered to have manners towards a fifteen-year-old.

'What's new with you, Paul?' asked Eoin.

'As it happens, plenty,' answered Paul. 'A crowd of us are going to do a project for next year's Young Scientist Exhibition. It's about patterns of water usage in Dublin. We'll be trying to see how the shortages like last summer's come about and what can be done about it.'

'Good for you,' said Nuala, 'it'll keep you off the streets anyway.'

'Better than rioting after football matches,' said Eoin.

'Ah, we have that organised. There'll be time for a few riots, provided we keep to our research schedule, our science teacher tells us.'

'Very good. Who's this expert organiser?' asked Nuala.

'Mr Leather Lips. He's very keen on young people having a rounded education.'

Finally Eoin said, 'Sorcha's inside. I think she's doing her homework. She's a bit grumpy. We're insisting on collecting her, and you too, after the disco tomorrow. I hope you don't mind.'

Nuala added, 'It'll interfere with your style, but it's tough being a kid, I know all about it.'

Paul was a bit embarrassed. 'Oh, no, Mrs Rafferty,' he said, too quickly, 'of course, that'll be fine. Fine. We don't mind a bit, honestly.'

'Speak for yourself,' advised Eoin, not unkindly, as Paul headed for the door.

'Am I interrupting the great scholar's concentration, the flow of the philosopher's thoughts?' he asked Sorcha.

'Actually, yes. Shouldn't you be off measuring the loss from leaky water taps? Did my mother tell you about her friend who left the tap on all night and flooded not only his apartment but the three on the floors below him as well? He's going to collect us, you know, tomorrow night.'

'The guy who left the tap on?'

'No, stupid, Dad.'

'I know. I told them that it was all right.'

'What? You told them it was all right? Blast you. You're just afraid to stand up to them.'

'That's not fair.'

'I've been fighting with them for two days about this and you come in doing the nice boy Paul who's everybody's parents' favourite. Yes, Mrs Rafferty. No, Mr Rafferty. I'll just lie down here and you can walk on me.'

Paul came around the table to where Sorcha was sitting and stood beside her. He put his arms around her and bent over her.

'You're very cross,' he said gently, 'what had you been planning for us?' He nuzzled his face against her.

'Well,' Sorcha said, relaxing a little, 'I had thought of this.' She turned and kissed him on the lips.

A moment later Paul murmured, 'I should have argued.' Sorcha said nothing. His tone changed, 'Ah well, there'll be other times. What are you doing there?'

Sorcha began to tell him about her essay but thought to herself that Paul was very easily placated. Did he not get frustrated when plans were upset or when things went wrong, the way she did?

6

Sorcha strolled between the trees and breathed deeply to clear her head. She was studying hard for the Inter and it was supposed to be a good idea to take breaks between subjects. She was looking forward to the summer, when it would all be over and she could relax. It seemed kind of funny, that the Inter was finishing. Hers was to be the last year of it before a new exam was introduced. The Intermediate Certificate of Education: even the name sounded funny, sort of old-fashioned, as if Martin Luther had probably done it. It seemed that she had always known of it. She remembered Conor doing his three years ago, and her parents often talked about their own Inter. When she finished, it would be all over, forever. She felt that the first and second years in school were new, belonged to a new age. It was funny that she knew nothing about the courses they were following. She wondered whether old people felt like that about teenagers.

It was getting dark as Sorcha walked by Miley's Place as they still thought of it although it had been occupied for about three months. The house had been tidied up and there were new plants in the front garden. They looked like vegetables to Sorcha but she was sure that nobody would plant vegetables in their front garden. As she was passing, the boy she had seen a few times before came down the path and out the gate. His hair was still long and untidy and he was still desperately thin. He had no haversack or climbing boots but he was carrying a satchel, made from some kind of cloth material.

'Hi,' said Sorcha, without thinking.

He looked up, as if surprised that she spoke. 'Hello,' he said, 'I'm Roger Darling.' He put out his hand.

Sorcha hesitated a moment and then reached out and shook it. It was the first time she had shaken hands with someone who was around her own age. 'Hello. I'm Sorcha Rafferty.'

'Yes,' said Roger. 'I've seen you.'

Sorcha was surprised that he had noticed. Any time she had seen him he had seemed completely involved in his own thoughts. He looked straight at her as he spoke to her. She did not really want to say anything else to him but he turned to walk in her direction. She could hardly turn back and say, 'Excuse me, I've finished my walk'.

They walked for a short while and Roger said nothing. He looked straight ahead and seemed to be paying no attention to Sorcha. She thought he might be shy. Whatever about him, she was feeling uncomfortable with the silence so she tried to think of something to say to him.

'Do you like living here then?'

'Well, it's interesting. Before this we lived in the country and we're not used to people's habits in the city. There's so much waste here, and the air is so dirty. People don't seem to notice.' He again looked straight at her with his blue eyes as he spoke. Sorcha felt that he was very serious, but not in a dull way like Frank. Maybe he wasn't shy at all. Once again he lapsed into silence. He did not seem to mind whether they talked or not.

She decided to try again. 'I've seen you going hiking.'

'Yes. I like to get to the mountains. Here it's too busy. You've no time for yourself. Everything rushes headlong. There it's unspoilt, if you go high enough, above the farms. You can think. You can discover yourself. Be yourself.'

Again he looked at her. He's certainly not shy, thought Sorcha. He's confident. They walked on, again in silence. After a few more moments he turned to her.

'What about you? Do you swim through life here in the city like a fish through water, taking it all for granted, never thinking about it, just like the others do?'

Sorcha decided not to be put off. 'What do you mean? Of course I think. I'm not stupid.'

'Good,' said Roger, 'I'm glad. But do you think about the lead you breathe in from all these cars.' He raised his arm slightly, indicating the passing traffic. 'Do you think about the toxins in your food?

'I suppose. We learn about it in school. There are other things to think about, you know.'

'Such as?' he asked. Sorcha felt that he was mocking her now. She felt uncomfortable. He was a lot older than her. She definitely did not want to seem stupid in front of him, not like a Simone. Alice Smith flashed into her mind. Definitely not an Alice, she said to herself.

'Such as my Inter,' Sorcha said. She immediately regretted it.

'Oh, you looked older than that,' said Roger.

Sorcha could feel his interest in her draining away, like water from a sink. 'I'm old beyond my years,' she said, feeling stupid.

'Yes,' he said. 'I go this way. I've got a meeting.' He patted his bag. Sorcha did not know why he did that.

'See you around.' She hesitated before using his name. 'Roger,' she said.

'Sure,' he said and walked off, lost again in his thoughts.

Sorcha went home but found it hard to concentrate on her study. Something about Roger had unsettled her. It was the way he seemed to be fully concentrating on you when he spoke to you, she thought. And the way he paid no attention when he did not. It also occurred to her that that was probably the first conversation she'd had with a boy other than Paul that didn't involve joke telling and slagging.

Roger Darling. What a stupid name, Sorcha decided.

7

Saturday afternoon was mild and breezy. April was almost over and the city was full of its growth. Blossoms, flowers, leaves, birds singing, scents, the expectation of a long peaceful evening serenaded to sleep by blackbirds in the trees filled the air and the ground and Sorcha's head. She held Paul's hand and felt that she was only half in contact with the ground. Gone was her winter coat, gone were her heavy shoes and socks, gone were hats and scarves and gloves. She was light and airy in jeans, tee-shirt and jumper, new runners on her feet, no bag, no books. She could forget, for a while, the Inter, just over five weeks away.

She turned to Paul and kissed him. 'I love spring,' she said. 'It's so ... ' she trailed off and tossed her hair. He grabbed her waist and lifted her. 'Light,' he said, finishing her sentence. Sorcha skipped down the road and Paul followed, laughing at her. 'Feel the breeze,' she called to him and twirled around, her hands high in the air. 'You're crazy,' he said, but joined her twirling, faster and faster until they flopped onto a bench, dizzy and convulsed by laughing. An old man, walking his dog, tut-tutted at them. Sorcha stuck her tongue out at his back. 'Silly faggot,' said Paul. 'I'm in too good a humour to retaliate or I'd go after him and bite his dog.'

Sorcha put her head on Paul's shoulder and snuggled up to him. They sat like that for a while, his arm around her shoulders, saying little. Sorcha liked the way they could relax, and not mind silence between them. Paul was just about to kiss her, she knew, when she said, 'I met Roger the other day.'

'Did you? Who's Roger?'

'You don't know Roger? Everyone knows Roger. He's special.' She could feel Paul tensing slightly. She didn't know why, but she was egging him on, wanted to annoy him, to make him jealous. It was some mischievous spirit of spring, perhaps. Wasn't spring a time for shaking up the old, for cleaning carpets and stuff, for new growth?

'Roger the Dodger,' she answered. 'Give us a kiss.' She turned to face him but paused. 'Roger Darling. He's really interesting. Mature. He's not a kid.'

'Roger darling! You must know him well.' Paul was trying to sound careless, as if he did not mind what Sorcha did.

'That's his name, stupid. Roger Darling.'

'What a stupid name,' said Paul. 'What's so "interesting" about him?'

'Well, he really looks at you, as if you're there, as if he's really listening.'

'I suppose I don't. I suppose I'm just a kid who knows nothing.'

'No, but, I mean if you put it like that .... He's into the environment and all.' Sorcha sensed that Paul was hurt and she wanted to withdraw. She decided to try to talk to him, direct.

'Look, Paul, what do you want, from me, from us, I mean?'

He was quiet, not knowing what to say.

'Is it true that all boys are "only interested in one thing"?'

'Do I seem like that to you?'

'Well, no, but I was wondering. They say it's so.'

'Who says? Parents? Teachers? What do they know? Some of them are, I mean, yes they might be, some boys. But I want more, I want ... Look, I don't know how to talk about it. It's not easy.' He looked at her.

Sorcha was sitting up straight now, facing him on the bench.

'I want to be close to you. I want to be your friend. I like your company. Yes, I like touching you and things. Of course I think about it. Don't you?' He was speaking very seriously and intensely.

'Yeh, of course, but not all the time. I think about other things too. You know, the environment, the air and stuff.' Sorcha realised that this was a little bit second-hand. It was what she should have said to Roger and then she wouldn't have seemed like a fool. 'Boys exploit girls. They use them. There's no use denying it.'

'Look, Sorcha, if that's all you think of me, forget it. I'm not going to be lumped in, categorised. I'm not Jeff. What about Simone? Isn't she exploiting boys?'

'She's a victim of circumstances.'

'Who told you that?'

'Look, we've had debates about this in school. I've thought about it.'

Paul was angry and upset, she could see that. She knew she wasn't being fair to him.

'How long have we been going out?'

'Two and a half months.'

'Have I tried anything?' Sorcha said nothing. 'Have I? With anyone else you'd be doing it.'

'No I would not, you swine.'

'Then he'd be gone.'

'Good riddance, if he was.'

'All I'm saying, Sorcha, is that I care about you. I like you.'

'I know. I like you too, you know. I'm just frisky in this weather. I'm being bad. I know you're not like that. Come on, give me a kiss.'

They tried, but their hearts were not in it. They got up and walked on. 'Roger is nobody, you know. I just said hello in the street. He's that half crazy self-deficient boy from the self-sufficient family in Miley's Place. I was only slagging you.'

'Some slag,' said Paul and put his arm around her.

During the week Sorcha met Roger again. She went towards Miley's Place not really thinking of Roger at all, though she noticed that she had called it Roger's Place in her mind. She supposed that that was more appropriate now. He was going into his house and they met near the gate. She was sure this time that some of the plants in the garden were potatoes.

'My goodness, Mr Smith, do you see what those dreadful Darling people have in their front garden?' 'No, dear, I don't.' 'Potatoes, Mr Smith, and parsnips and carrots.' 'Potatoes. My goodness. Make a few quid, eh? Maybe we should try it ourselves, dear,' Mr Smith joked. 'Oh, dear, you're so funny, dear,' said Mrs Smith. 'Oh, Daddy, don't. It's so awful even to think about it,' said Alice Smith, deeply shocked. 'Parsnips,' said Simon Smith, plotting secretly as usual.

'Hello, Roger,' said Sorcha, 'How's it going?' She felt nervous, suddenly.

'Hello there ... Sorcha, isn't it?' said Roger. Sorcha was surprised that he had remembered her name.

'No meeting tonight?' she asked, to keep the conversation going a little longer. For some reason she felt she wanted to impress Roger. She kept remembering her silly answers the last time they met and the way he reacted when he heard that she was only doing the Inter.

'Ah, yes, I was going to a meeting the last time we met. That was a little matter not resolved. Things can't be allowed to continue. It's only a matter of time before the planet won't be able to sustain life.' He was looking straight at her, his whole attention on her.

Sorcha felt that she must respond. 'Progress is being made,' she said, 'Look at the green products you can buy now.'

'True,' said Roger, still looking at her, 'but that's not enough. It's the tip of the iceberg. Half the time they're not even any good, those products.'

'I know. My mum bought a floor cleaner and it was useless. I ended up scrubbing the floor on my hands and knees,' she laughed.

Roger did not. 'That's not what I mean. They're often as harmful as the ones they replace. And they're in plastic bottles. How stupid. Anyhow, things will have to change. We're messing with conservation now, fiddling a little with this and that. If we're to survive we'll all have to consume less, use less of everything, fuel, the lot. We'll, all of us, have to get down on our knees and scrub.' He smiled at her when he said this, a short smile that disappeared again nearly before it was fully grown.

He was just about to start talking again when Sorcha decided to interrupt. The last thing she wanted was to seem as if she had nothing to say for herself. 'You know, Roger, I've thought that same thought myself sometimes. We can't just use resources indiscriminately.' Sorcha tried to look at Roger as intensely as he looked at her but had to turn away. She did think that what she said sounded impressive enough, although she had no intention of getting down and breaking her back again to scrub the floor. She had made her mother buy the old cleaner after her one bad experience.

'Exactly,' he said. He actually did look impressed. He seemed to Sorcha to become more intense then, if that was possible. He leaned towards her slightly, ready to speak. She felt that she had passed some test, that he was about to take her into his confidence. 'There are so many issues,' he said, 'but right now we have to think of dolphins. Do you know that in the Pacific Ocean yellowfin tuna swim beneath the herds of dolphin? In the past local fishing boats caught tuna and it was consumed locally but then the big industries took over. They have dozens of ships. They encircle a herd of dolphin with their nets and then pull them tight. The tuna underneath are caught. Object achieved. What they don't care about, because they don't see this planet as an ecological system where all life is interwoven, is that the dolphins drown when they get caught in the nets. Soon they'll all be gone. As long as there's profit they don't care. They're also stupid. They're fishing so intensely that the tuna stocks are being depleted. If they go on they'll reach the critical point and will become extinct in the area. Profit will be gone then anyway, and so will the dolphins.'

Roger stopped. Sorcha felt as if she had just listened to a lecture. Roger was a good lecturer and while he spoke he waved his arms for emphasis, totally absorbed in what he was saying. Sorcha didn't know what to say. 'How awful' or 'really' would definitely sound stupid, after having obviously made some impression on him.

'What can we do?' she asked.

That seemed to please him. 'That's what we've been meeting about. There are possibilities. What we need is a complete ban on imports of tuna, but that's at international level. Locally we can educate people, we can protest. If you're really interested...' He left his sentence hanging and waited for her to respond.

'I am, I am,' said Sorcha. But she was not at all sure.

What was certain was that the next time she found tuna on her plate she literally could not eat it. She had gone off particular foods before, spaghetti for instance, but then there'd been no obvious reason. Now there was. She could not get the dolphins out of her mind. She actually liked tuna, always enjoyed it. But she had seen TV programmes on dolphins and knew how intelligent and friendly they were, and how harmless. A girl in her class had been to see Fungi, the Dingle dolphin in Kerry. He seemed almost human. People were devoted to him. She couldn't accept the idea of dolphins being killed so she could put this stuff on her plate. Sorcha had a sympathetic attraction to anything intelligent, just as she could never be interested in anything stupid. She ate no lunch that day. In her house if you didn't eat what was there, you ate nothing. That was the rule.

8

Sorcha was fed up with any mention of the Inter. Every teacher in every class reminded them of it at least five times. Then she had to go home, do hours of homework and then hours of study. Sometimes she felt it would be better to abandon the whole business. She knew her parents expected her to do well, to go to university. She expected it herself. No one in her house had ever even imagined that anything else could happen. It was only now, for the first time, that the idea of leaving school presented itself to Sorcha, even as a remote possibility. Conor was encouraging about study, when she saw him. He told her that university was great fun, really adult with plenty of freedom. But he was still doing exams and studying as well. On top of that she still had two more years of school before university.

It wasn't really worry about the exams that was upsetting her though. She had studied all along and was well prepared. It was Roger who was causing the problem. Not Roger himself but what he had said to her. She could not get it out of her mind. She had told her parents about the tuna and the dolphins, without telling them where she had heard it. They probably supposed that she learnt it in school. They always took very seriously what she learnt in school. It was part of their strategy for encouraging her in her education. Neither of them had heard of the dolphin kills before.

'It's typical really,' Eoin said. 'We don't really need tuna fish. Yet we're convinced we do so that a few will get rich. And the planet suffers. Are we all mad, crazy?'

'Oh, Dad, you're right. I was talking to ...' Sorcha paused briefly, not wanting to introduce Roger to the conversation. She was having a funny reaction to Roger which she did not really understand herself, and she didn't want to answer questions about him at the moment. 'I was talking to someone the other day who was saying just that. The whole of the environment, all the species are being destroyed.'

'Well, at least we can do something about the tuna,' Nuala said. 'Let's not get it anymore.'

Sorcha was surprised at how easy the decision was. She felt defiant, bold, strong really. Yes, they would challenge the might of these heartless people by not buying their product. She was delighted. She felt like kissing her mother.

'Oh, can we do that? Dad, what do you think?'

'I think, yes, we must. We could also write to the Department of Industry and Commerce about it.'

'And to the Department of the Environment,' added Nuala.

So the ban on tuna fish came into effect in the Rafferty household. Sorcha felt a slight niggling of conscience that Conor had not been there to be involved, but she put it out of her mind, by reminding herself that he was hardly ever there and so was hardly part of the family.

* * *

Sorcha was rarely outside, except for school, so she did not meet the gang very often. On Saturday afternoon, though, they were hanging around, those preparing for exams full of talk about them, the rest full of relief. Pam was there, and Frank and Jeff and Molly and Paul.

After a while, to change the subject, Sorcha said, 'We've banned tuna in our house.'

Jeff said, 'Is he very rough, or what, Sorcha?'

Molly added, 'Why on earth, Sorcha? Explain yourself.'

'If Sorcha has done this there must be a very good reason. Has there been some scare about toxins, or is it political in some way, South Africa or something?' asked Frank, interested at once in something weighty.

Paul decided to take Jeff's tone, 'No, Frank, it's more serious than that. This fellow, Tuna O'Malley, has been calling 'round to Rafferty's. He says it's part of a study he's doing for a university degree but really it's because he fancies Sorcha like mad. Anyway, he drinks something awful and turned up drunk two nights ago. Sorcha's father confronted him in the hall and drew himself up to his full height and said, "Tuna O'Malley, you bounder. You've been studying my daughter. You are banned. Banned I say, forthwith. Leave my ..." '

He had to stop then because Pam grabbed him under the arms and tickled him. 'Shut up, dumb-bell. That's a stupid story.' But she was laughing. Paul caught her hands. 'Be careful, Pamela, or you will suffer.' He managed to twist her arms behind her and took hold of her wrists with one hand. With the other he tickled her ribs. Jeff shouted, 'Knights to the rescue,' and jumped on Paul, pulling him away. 'Flee, O damsel,' he called to Pam, 'I have rescued you.'

'Fleabag yourself,' said Pam, 'I didn't ask to be rescued. We were having fun, weren't we Paul?'

'Indeed we were,' said Paul.

They were all laughing and Paul looked at Sorcha to see how she was taking the fooling between him and Pam. She was laughing but at the same time she was a bit irritated, although not because of that. She did not own Paul. She had been serious about telling all of them about the tuna, though, and wanted them to listen. Frank came to her aid when he asked to hear more about the ban. The others listened for a few moments while she explained about the dolphins but were still giddy.

'Flipper the bush kangaroo,' sang Jeff, as off key as could be.

'Shut up,' said Pam. 'Sorcha, this is serious. What do you hope to get out of it?'

'Get out of it? Come off it. Everything can't be for what we get out of it. There's an issue here.'

Frank said, 'It's important, all right, I can see that. But your ban won't help much will it?'

'What about jobs? Jobs in fishing are important. If you don't eat the fish what will the fishermen do?' Molly asked.

'Molly, don't be silly. People will get other jobs. We're talking here about a species of animal.'

'Yes, but ...' began Molly.

'Has the whole family agreed?' asked Paul, interrupting her.

'Yeh.'

'Conor as well?'

'Yes, of course,' said Sorcha, feeling that it was easier to say this than offer a longer and fuller explanation.

'I bet Roger is at the bottom of this,' said Paul, his tone light-hearted, but glancing at Sorcha nonetheless.

'Who's Roger?' they all asked, more or less at once.

'Roger Darling. That weirdo who grows onions in his front garden at Miley's Place. He's one of those environment freaks. He'd have us eating boiled lentils and using horses instead of cars and recycling their dung.'

'And living by candlelight,' said Jeff.

'And doing away with packages,' said Pam.

'And no more washing our hair,' said Molly.

'And recycling toothpaste,' said Jeff.

'And telling stories instead of watching telly,' said Paul.

'And bartering,' said Pam.

'And using no toilet paper,' said Jeff.

'And no jobs,' said Molly.

'Oh, shut up, the lot of you,' shouted Sorcha, more exasperated than annoyed. 'You're all so smarty assed. You don't see things, you don't care about anything.'

'We do,' said Pam. 'We're having fun, Sorcha, that's all. It's not the end of the world.' She paused. 'Yet!'

They all laughed: even Sorcha grinned.

'I'm going home,' she said, 'study calls.'

'I'll walk with you,' said Paul.

'Yes, do,' said Sorcha.

On the way home she asked him what he thought about it all. Paul was sure that she was right but he could not take it all that seriously. If you could not laugh, it seemed to him, it wouldn't matter whether or not there were dolphins. Sorcha saw his point but still felt exasperated that only she could see the seriousness of the issue. She wondered what Roger would think, and could not imagine him laughing at it at all.

* * *

During the week, on the way home from school, Sorcha met Roger. Rather, he seemed to be waiting for her, so she supposed that he met her. He invited her to a meeting later that week to plan the campaign about the tuna. Sorcha was so flabbergasted to be asked that she accepted straight away, even though she didn't really have time to spare. She arranged to meet Roger outside his house (suddenly no longer Roger's Place in her mind) on Thursday evening at seven. On the way home she wondered what her parents would say, and knew that they would not be pleased.

* * *

When Thursday came she told her mother that there was a meeting about the environment, managed to leave the impression it was in school and got out before there were too many questions. She rushed around to Roger's house. He was waiting.

'Well!' said Sorcha, as bright and cheery as possible, although she felt apprehensive about the meeting, and about being with Roger. She thought briefly about Paul and wondered whether he'd mind. She supposed she'd have to tell him.

'You're late,' said Roger, looking at his watch. 'We've to be there at half seven.'

'It's only two minutes past. Can we take the bus? Where are we going?' Sorcha decided not to be apologetic about herself.

She was a bit in awe of Roger but he wasn't going to boss her about.

'No. We'll walk. Walking is the best way to travel,' said Roger, starting out.

'Yes, that's true, but if it was the only way we'd all be stuck in the middle ages.'

'Look, are you serious about this or not?' He turned and looked at her with his very intense expression.

Sorcha was uncomfortable. She felt that she was here under false pretences, at least partly. Roger had somehow picked up the notion that she was much more concerned about the environment than she actually was. She was not sure at all why she was going to this meeting. Her maths homework, undone and very long, flashed before her - like a drowning person's life might, she thought. Don't exaggerate, she chided herself, in her head.

'Yes, I'm serious. I wouldn't be here if I wasn't.' As she said it she suddenly knew that she really did care, it was not just an act to impress him. 'But, Roger, I'm not as well up on it as you. I really have a lot to learn. We ban products in our house, you know, ones that aren't acceptable,' she said and then added, 'like tuna.'

'Huh, that stuff's not real food. Nothing that comes from a factory is. Anyway it's meat. I'm surprised you have to ban it at all. Vegetables, organically grown. That's the way to use the land economically. You do have a lot to learn. We walk.'

Sorcha had half hoped that Roger would not pick up her remark about the tuna. She no longer felt so pleased with herself about it. Suddenly it felt silly, amateurish to her.

9

They arrived at an ordinary suburban house after about twenty minutes. There were eight other people there, all a good deal older than her and Sorcha was very uncomfortable and embarrassed. Be cool she urged herself. At least she had not dressed up, was wearing jeans and runners, as were all the others.

Some sat on chairs, the rest on the floor. Roger seemed to be in charge. He explained that they were there to organise a campaign in Dublin to highlight the problems of dolphins and tuna fish in the Pacific Ocean. He asked for ideas. Sorcha tried to remember the people Roger had introduced her to.

'Look,' said a boy called Eoin, who seemed about twenty. He was fair haired, tall and good looking. 'The scene is this. The big companies, the multi-nationals, have a stake in everything. They own the canneries, the boats, they own farms. They're even into other things, electronics and so on. Tuna means nothing to them. Zilch. They don't care. Profit. Lots of it. They destroy forests for hamburgers. People for slave wages. I'd like to blast them all.'

Then a girl called Brenda spoke. She was about nineteen and her eyes blazed. Sorcha had never understood what blazing eyes meant until she saw Brenda.

'Do you know that salmon fishing is as bad? The Japanese use drift nets and kill porpoises with them. They abandon their broken nets, clogging up the ocean. Thousands of birds get entangled.'

Sorcha thought she was beautiful. She was filled with real, deep anger about what she was saying.

'If this goes on there'll soon be enough of these old nets in the water to go one third of the way around the world. One third. Just imagine. Think of the damage. Who cares?' Her voice rose as she looked around at them all. 'Do you know what they call them? Ghost nets! Appropriate isn't it?'

At the last words Brenda laughed but Sorcha knew she was not amused. As they spoke she knew that her own gesture of not eating tuna would be laughed at here. They were way beyond that.

'Well, really!' said Mrs Smith, in her most shocked voice. The other Smiths seemed to have abandoned Sorcha and she knew that even Mrs Smith wasn't going to be of much use here. These were serious people.

'Do you know,' Eoin began again, 'that the food we import from the Third World, fruit, coffee and so on, has toxins in it that we ban here.'

Sorcha was not sure what he was talking about but could not have stopped herself listening.

'Pesticides are used in Latin America and Africa that have been outlawed here for years, such as DDT. The multi-nationals use them there though for more profit, because there are no laws to stop them.'

His voice, like Brenda's a short while before, filled with outrage.

'The workers in the fields don't even wear protective clothes. They're not told of the danger.' He stopped, to increase the effect of what he was going to say. 'And we import the stuff. We'd ban it if it was home produced. They have us all screwed. Screwed.'

They know so much, thought Sorcha. There was another girl of about twenty with long, wavy hair and dark clothes sitting on the floor who said, 'Look, the whole political scene is very complicated. Maybe too complicated for this meeting, with so many at it.' Sorcha remembered that Roger had said that her name was Olivia. She felt that she was referring to Sorcha herself, because she was new and an outsider.

'You're right,' said Roger. 'Some people are here only because of the dolphins. One issue people.' He smiled.

'That's not true,' someone said.

'Only joking,' said Roger. So, he can joke, thought Sorcha. She realised that Roger had faded into the background of her mind while she listened to the others. She would have liked to hear more of their comments.

'So, let's discuss the leaflets,' said Roger. The plan, it turned out, was to prepare leaflets and petition forms to distribute in the city centre and at shopping centres every Saturday for a month. They discussed the content of the leaflets, the wording of the petition and the printing of the material. Sorcha said nothing.

Finally they came to the handing out of the leaflets. Roger turned to her for the first time, and said, 'Sorcha, can you and some of your friends help here, on Saturdays? Handing them out, I mean.' Everyone turned to look at her, expectantly. She could feel herself blushing and was sure it was obvious to them all.

'I've got,' she nearly said, 'my Inter', which would have given her age away but she caught herself and instead said, 'exams coming up.'

'Sorcha's doing her Inter,' said Roger. 'Don't worry, Sorcha, it will take a few weeks to organise. You'll be finished. Are you in?'

Sorcha was sure she looked like a tomato and said, 'Yes,' to get the attention away from her.

* * *

On the way home she said to Roger, 'You're rotten, you really are. There was no need to tell them that I was only doing the Inter.'

'What's wrong with that? You are who you are. There's nothing wrong with being fourteen.'

'Fifteen,' corrected Sorcha.

'Fifteen either. You have to learn to accept yourself. Your strengths and your weaknesses. Don't try to be someone you're not.' He was fixing her with his gaze again.

Afterwards, she thought about what he had said but she also wondered whether he invited her along only because she had friends who could hand out leaflets - mere foot soldiers. Sorcha wanted to be taken more seriously than that. Of that she was sure, dead sure.

* * *

The next day, at dinner, she could feel the tension in the air. It was always like that when her parents wanted to talk to her about something serious.

'Sorcha.'

'Yes, Dad.'

'What was that meeting about, in school, last night?'

Sorcha thought that she heard a slight emphasis on 'in school'. She wondered whether they'd been talking to someone else's parents and knew that there had been no such meeting. She decided truth was the best course of action. After all she had only misled them in the first place to avoid awkward explanations, not to deceive anyone.

'Look, Dad, Mom, it wasn't actually a meeting in school.'

'What do you mean "actually", Sorcha?' asked Nuala, with forced restraint.

'Well, it was a meeting, I mean, I was at a meeting. It just wasn't in school, that's all. See?'

'No, we don't see,' said Eoin.

We. We. We. Why is it always we? Sorcha asked in her head. The Smiths stood up straight, together, linking arms, facing adversity. The only flaw was Simon, kicking Alice behind everyone's back.

'Well,' said Sorcha miserably, 'it was a meeting about the environment, that's all.'

'Yes, but where was it?' asked her mother.

'Well, it was in someone's house. I'm not sure of the address, actually.'

'Is this a group of some sort? Is it An Taisce?' asked her mother.

'No. Well, yes. It's a group. It's not An Taisce.' Sorcha didn't know what An Taisce was.

'What is it then? Greenpeace? Earthwatch? For God's sake, Sorcha, tell us what's going on?' said Eoin, angry now.

She knew about Greenpeace and Earthwatch all right.

'No. It's not those. It's just a small group. Roger invited me.'

'Who's Roger?'

'Roger Darling. He lives nearby. He's into that sort of thing.'

'What sort of thing? What about Paul? What does he think?'

'I thought you wanted me to mix, to have lots of friends. Anyway it's not like that. It's about the environment.'

'We do,' said her mother, 'but you must be sensible. What sort of fellow is Roger?'

'Oh, he's old.' She could see her parents disturbed by that. 'No, he's not that old. He's not a dirty old man or anything. He's serious. I don't fancy him or anything.'

'What about your Inter?' said Eoin.

'Oh, Dad, it was only one night.'

'Yes, but the exams are so close, Sorcha. You only get one chance.'

'Oh, Eoin, she's well prepared. Let's not worry her about that, at this stage.'

'I suppose. All the same,' said Eoin.

'I suppose that's where you got the idea about the tuna?' asked her mother.

'Well, yes. Look, it's serious. It's not only tuna anyway. We must be involved.'

'I know,' said Eoin, 'but be careful. We worry about you. You'll have to find out more about this group. We want to know what you're doing, that's all.'

* * *

Sorcha got into bed feeling that it had not gone too badly. They hadn't banned her, or unbanned tuna fish. The next step was to convince the gang to hand out leaflets. She was working out what to say to them when she fell asleep.

10

Everyone went wild. Groups raced up and down the streets shouting and cheering. They arranged outings and parties. Some were going to the beach for the day and then partying all night. There was a general air of craziness in the city. The Inter was over.

Sorcha said, 'One thing for sure, this whole thing is exaggerated.'

'What do you mean?'

'Look, it's only the Inter we've finished.'

'I know, but isn't it great?' Pam shouted the last word and twirled about, her arms in the air. She ran over to Sorcha and hugged her.

'Mar-vell-ous,' shouted Sorcha and they spun around madly. The sky, blue and clear for over a week, spun dizzily above their heads. They laughed and clung to each other until they couldn't stand. They flopped onto the pavement, their backs to a garden wall. Sorcha was panting. 'It's over.' There were students from other schools about who were usually ignored and when they passed they gave friendly waves or called across the street.

After a while Pam asked, 'What'll we do tonight?'

Sorcha was quiet for a while, then said, 'Pam, what I was saying earlier, you know, it's only the Inter. We're back to school in September. It's not really the end of anything. The Leaving'll be a million times harder. It's a relief it's over, sure. But I don't feel like going wild because of it.'

'Everyone else will be having fun,' said Pam.

'Look, you know people like Martina. "I'll be having a few pints with David later on, quiet celebration, you know".' Sorcha was imitating her affected accent. 'They'll be out getting drunk. I'd be killed.'

'So would I. Dead. My father ranted and raved about the messing last year.'

'Mine as well, and my Mom. You should have heard her. Pam, let's go to the pictures and get a burger. Forget the rest.'

'OK, you're right, let's.'

* * *

Later Sorcha met Paul. 'I thought I wouldn't see you tonight,' he said. 'I thought you'd be on the town.'

'Naw, too unsophisticated for Sorcha, that,' she answered. 'Anyway, Paul, there's too much of it.'

'I agree. Absolutely. Definitely. You are one hundred percent, no let me correct that, one hundred and forty percent right, Sorcha. Too much of what, exactly?'

'Too much fuss about the Inter. Everyone overdoes things.'

'What things? Celebrating?' Paul remembered his own celebration the year before. He hadn't come home until three in the morning and there had been an almighty row. At least he had not been drinking, like some of his classmates.

'Everything. Everyone overdoes everything.'

'No. I don't,' Paul said and grabbed Sorcha and began kissing her. 'See,' he said, stopping abruptly, to demonstrate his restraint.

'Paul, you're driving me mad. I'm trying to talk, to think. Then I was just starting to enjoy kissing you and you've stopped.'

'Think away.'

'Look, I've been thinking. One of the problems with the world, you know one of the things that this conservation is all about, is that we overdo everything. We eat too much, we use too much stuff. We'll have to cut back, the world will, or we won't survive.'

'What's that got to do with the Inter?' Paul asked, quite reasonably, he thought.

'Well, can't you see? They all overdo the celebrations, there's too much of them. It's not ...' Sorcha paused, looking for a word, 'appropriate.'

'What's that got to do with conservation?' Paul asked, quite reasonably, he thought.

'Nothing. It's a symptom.'

'A what? This isn't a sickness. It's fun. You used to like fun.'

'I do. But it's too much. We're all, the world, in the habit of too much. We don't rely on ourselves any more. We don't have enough acceptance of ourselves. We need all these things, the things we consume to fill the gap.'

'Mmm,' said Paul.

'Look, I just feel the Inter thing is like that a bit as well.'

'OK, you may be right.' Paul did not sound at all convinced.

'Look, can we just drop it, can we. You don't understand.'

'I do. In fact I agree with you. I want to help, to be involved.'

Sorcha had told Paul about her meeting with Roger and his friends. She thought that he was probably a bit jealous. He had asked her about Roger again but she had assured him that it was only an organisation, nothing else, nothing personal.

'I know you do,' she said, 'but you have to be asked to join. I told you that.'

She asked him about the leaflets and he thought it was a good idea. They agreed to put the plan to the gang together.

* * *

They met Simone, Pam, Smiley-Joe, Jeff, Frank and Molly. They were walking through the streets with nothing to do. Sorcha decided to try them with the idea of the leaflets.

'Hey, isn't this boring.' There was a chorus of agreement. 'I've got a brilliant idea.' Everyone waited, expectantly. 'Remember I was telling you about dolphins and tuna a while ago?'

Jeff said, 'Yeh, I remember. A while ago. Flipper, Flipper the bush kangaroo,' he sang. 'You got in an awful strunt Sorchee-Worchee.'

'Oh my God, he's off again,' said Sorcha.

'What's Flipper got to do with tuna fish?' asked Molly.

'He's a dolphin,' explained Smiley-Joe.

'But Jeff's singing about a kangaroo,' said Molly, sounding confused.

Jeff put his arm around Molly's shoulders, walked her slightly away from the others and began to talk to her in an exaggeratedly patient voice so that everyone could hear, 'Molly, it's a joke. That's when you say something silly so that other people will laugh. Now...'

Molly realised that she was being made fun of so she pulled herself away and hit Jeff on the shoulder. 'You're horrible,' she said.

'What about the dolphins anyway?' asked Pam.

'Well, you know that group that Roger's in? Well, they're protesting about the killing of the dolphins to catch tuna. They're going to be handing out leaflets on Saturdays for the next month or so. They'd like us to help them.'

'Oh, wow, Sorcha baby, you don't mean it. Wowee, how exciting. Boy, that'll be the end of boredom for all time.' Jeff danced around and said the last few words in a very deep and serious voice.

'Actually, it might be no harm to do something useful for once,' said Sorcha.

'I think it might be fun,' said Smiley-Joe.

'Will Roger's friend be there, the one with the blond hair?' asked Simone. She had been curious about Roger and had seen him going in and out of his house a few times.

'I'm sure he will,' said Sorcha.

'I'm in,' said Simone, automatically touching her hair. She's going on duty at the thought of a man, Sorcha thought.

Paul said, 'Why don't we try it? It might be interesting seeing how people take to us. And it is a good cause.'

After a few minutes' persuasion, the gang agreed to give it a try.

* * *

Saturday morning found Sorcha, Paul, Pam, Simone, Molly, Jeff and Smiley-Joe in O'Connell Street, beside the huge stone columns at the GPO. It was a quarter to ten.

'I arranged to meet them at ten,' said Sorcha, 'and with them it's better not to be late. Being organised is part of their way of life.'

The GPO was a place where people often came to try to convince others of their ideas. One middle-aged man was sitting on a stool, wrapped in a blanket. On the window-ledge behind him stood a row of fruit, an apple, an orange, a banana, a kiwi, a pear and a few others. He had no placard or leaflets and was making no attempt to stop passers by, or talk to anyone. He was slowly eating a peach, the juice running down his chin. Some of the fruit looked a bit old and there were a few gaps in the line, where some pieces had been removed and eaten. The man looked tired, as if he had been there for a long time. On the other side stood the man selling the republican newspaper, who seemed to be always there in the same place. Out on the pavement the young people with clipboards were trying to stop passers by, to get them to buy lines for charity. The street was beginning to get crowded.

Roger arrived. He was with the girl from the meeting, Brenda, and a man whom Sorcha had not seen before. He looked older than the others. They carried wrapped parcels. 'Hello, Sorcha,' said Roger looking around at the gang in his usual way, which Sorcha still found unsettling. 'Is this it then?' Sorcha was not sure if he was disappointed or simply not surprised that her friends were what he had expected. He seemed to make judgements about people very quickly and she could tell that to him her friends were nothing but ordinary conventional kids who would grow into ordinary conventional adults and never change anything. Sorcha glanced at the others and said to herself that Roger was right, that Jeff, Molly, Simone, Smiley-Joe were nothing special, were quite boring really. Frank was the only one who was at all interesting. He had not come with them, although he thought that the idea was good. He had no interest in anything practical, only in books, which she supposed made him boring as well. Pam, she said, Pam is all right. Even as she thought this, she wondered, really, in what way was Pam different from the others. Paul got included in this disloyal run of thought, despite Sorcha's efforts to keep him out of it. The thought began to worm its way into her mind: why was she going with Paul, if he was dull and boring and conventional? Roger had picked her out as someone special, above the others, apart. Another question niggled away at her: was he just using her, to get someone boring to help with the boring jobs?

Brenda said, 'Hi, Sorcha. How are you?' She stood beside her and they talked quietly about the day's work for a few moments. Sorcha was pleased by Brenda's warmth towards her. She had felt the same at the meeting, as if she was very sincere. She seemed to concentrate all her attention on you when she was talking to you but in a way that was welcoming and friendly and really interested. Sorcha was again impressed with her confidence. The way she stood as she talked to her, lightly putting her hand on Sorcha's arm, the way she looked about, tall and gorgeous, tossing her hair now and then made Sorcha think of a goddess.

Roger introduced himself to the gang. Sorcha kicked herself as soon as he started. She should have done that instead of talking to Brenda. He introduced the other man as George. Simone was put out because Roger's blond friend, Eoin, had not come along but she recovered quickly and slid up to George. He was tall and muscular and there was a streak of grey hair over each of his temples, giving him a mature look which appealed to Simone. She stood almost on top of George and looked him straight in the eye.

'I think what you're doing is wonderful, George, really wonderful. It's so ... ' she paused, as if searching for the right word, but actually doing it just for the effect, as part of her style. Sorcha bet herself that this was the wrong approach here. These people were strong, and tough. Simone went on, 'It's so ... important.' She emphasised 'important' as if it was a wonderful insight. George, who was at least ten years older than her, took advantage of his height to look over her head instead of at her. All he said was, 'Yes,' pointedly uninterested in her. Simone shrank away in disgust.

The Smiths appeared for a moment. Mr and Mrs were scowling. They did not approve of this behaviour. 'Hippies,' they muttered together. 'Why can't they get jobs like everyone else? Put us all out of work.' Mrs Smith sniffed. Sorcha winked at them. 'I won my bet,' she told them. Alice gasped. 'Betting,' was all she could manage to get out. Simon brightened, on cue.

George turned to Roger. 'Let's go then. We might as well start, if this is the best there is.'

'I know,' said Roger, 'but what can you do?'

The others were a few feet away, by the Post Office wall, and didn't hear but Sorcha was beside them, where she had been talking to Brenda and could not miss the comments. She felt a jab in her stomach. Roger and the rest did not care at all about them. It was as she had thought: that they were useful and, it seemed, only second rate useful at that. She had no intention of continuing in any group that thought of her in such a way. These were her friends, and even if they had limitations, they liked her and she liked them. At least they were straight with each other. As soon as this leafleting was over she was out. She could form her own environment group at school.

Simone had rejoined the others. She spoke to Paul, 'Mr Big Head over there thinks he's it. His nose is far too big for his face anyway, and look at his hair. It's primitive. And his clothes. Bet he hasn't been out of those jeans in years.' Paul looked at George, and whatever about Simone's other criticisms, had to agree that his nose was noticeably out of proportion with the rest of his face.

George, Roger and Brenda opened the parcels and gave each of them a bundle of leaflets. The gang read them. Then George quickly explained the problem so that they could answer any questions if they were asked. He also had petition forms and gave a clipboard to Paul, and one to Pam. He wanted them to get signatures, as many as possible. He then said that he wanted to take Pam, Molly and Jeff to College Green and get them to work there. They would meet up again later for coffee. They were all disappointed because they wanted the fun of being together. They could sensibly see, though, that they would target more people in two locations. They were also shy of objecting. 'Is that OK then?' asked George. It sounded more like an order than a question. Everyone answered, 'Yes.'

As they prepared to go, Roger slipped over to Sorcha. He said, so that only she could hear, 'Look, Sorcha, I wasn't including you, a minute ago. George is just a bit surprised you're all so young, that's all. But you're OK. Old beyond your years.' He smiled. 'OK?'

Sorcha tried to keep cool. Nothing that she had thought about Roger a few minutes ago had changed. But she knew, really, that it had. She was in. She was accepted. She had been right about Simone and the others. They were dull. As the others left for College Green she began to hand out her leaflets. Paul came over and asked her what Roger had said to her. 'Nothing,' she said, but got the feeling that Paul was not too happy being put off with that explanation.

They all gave out the first few leaflets without saying anything to the people. It was a bit embarrassing, now that they had started. Some people pretended not to see them, some took the leaflets and said thanks and others refused them. They all looked at these first ones, to see how they reacted. A few glanced at the papers and then crumpled them into the bins. Others shoved them in their pockets without reading them. More were thrown on the ground. Hardly anyone seemed to read them carefully. No one went to Paul to sign the petition. After a short time Sorcha noticed that more people were taking leaflets from Simone than from either herself or Smiley-Joe. Very few, in fact, refused her at all. Simone is very good looking and does know how to use it, she conceded jealously. Smiley-Joe smiled and thanked everyone who passed.

Two Gardaí came along and Simone asked the others, 'Do we need a licence for this?' Sorcha didn't know, hadn't even thought of it. Look natural,' she said. To herself she added, some chance, Simone baby! The Gardaí glanced at them but passed by. They were deep in conversation. 'All clear,' smiled Smiley-Joe.

A short distance away the two people with clipboards were starting to look over at them. The boy came over and said to Paul, 'Hey, this is our patch. We work it every Saturday. You're interfering with our business.'

Paul answered, 'We're not selling anything. It's only leaflets.'

'Yeh well, people aren't stopping for us because of you. Get lost.' He went back to his friend.

Paul told the others what he had said. They decided to ignore him. After a while he came back. This time he spoke to Sorcha. 'I told your friend to get lost. Now, for the last time, go away, or there'll be trouble. Blasted do-gooders.'

Sorcha said, 'Hey, you're selling for charity, what does that make you?'

He replied, 'Yeh, but we get a cut. We make money for this. You don't think that we do it for love?' He turned to Smiley-Joe and said, very aggressively, 'Hey you, go home to your mammy.'

Smiley-Joe was taken aback but he answered, 'We're not doing you any harm. We're only handing out leaflets.'

Clipboard almost yelled, 'I told you to get lost.' He grabbed at Smiley-Joe's shirt, but Smiley-Joe, to the others' surprise, dodged skilfully out of his reach and shouted at him, 'Leave me alone, or I'll call the Guards.'

Sorcha came over. 'You'll lose your licence, then you'll have no customers at all.'

He turned to her. 'Shut up and go home.'

'No,' answered Sorcha. 'I think I'll go to the post office and ring the Guards instead. No licence, no money. Now, will you leave us alone. We'll do our best not to interfere with you.'

The mention of the Guards had its effect and he went back to his friend. They spoke together before restarting their selling. Every now and again, they looked over at Sorcha and the others.

'They're not finished yet,' said Paul. It was only half ten.

Sorcha half-watched the line sellers as she passed out her leaflets. Each had an identical approach, learned on a course, she supposed. They picked on a passer by, the girl nearly always selecting men, the boy women, and with clipboards held at their sides, still in view but not too obvious, they began walking, half backwards, half sideways beside their victim. They smiled widely and greeted the person. If the walker did not stop they walked beside them for a few paces. Once or twice they came close enough to Sorcha for her to hear them. 'Really, I'll only take a second of your time. I just want to talk to you for a minute, that's all.' Sometimes, if the person walked on they began to thank them, full of sarcasm, their parting shot. If the intended victim, exasperated, told them to go away they often got aggressive and abusive, an approach which Sorcha presumed they did not learn on their course, and was their own innovation. If the walker stopped they were sugary sweet and swung the clipboard up into full action position, produced the pen and sold a line. Sorcha noticed that anyone who stopped was finished. It was impossible, then, to refuse. Out came the pound, flashing in the June sun. The only defence was to stay on the move and to avoid the ambush completely. 'This,' said Sorcha to Simone, 'is better than that,' indicating the clipboarders. 'Sure thing,' agreed Simone.

A man in his thirties, tall enough to be seen above the O'Connell Street crowds came down the steps of Eason's bookshop. He turned in their direction, after looking the other way first. He sauntered, obviously in no hurry, enjoying the warmth. The female clipboard was already closing on a prey so the male one approached, ready for the kill. He started on his patter, smiling, fawning, sideways walking. The older man spoke briefly, refusing him. Clipboard crabwalked, insistent. The man again refused. They were now within earshot of Sorcha who had moved towards the clipboards' space without noticing herself doing it. Clipboard said, getting irritated, sensing failure, 'Look, there's no need to be rude. I only want to talk to you for a minute, that's all.' The man stopped and looked directly at clipboard for the first time. 'Well I don't want to "talk to you", as you put it. I want to walk along this pavement. I want to think my thoughts. I don't want to be sold anything by a silly twit who prances up to me uninvited. Now, go away and leave me alone.' Clipboard stopped, unable to speak. Sorcha couldn't hide her laughter. 'Try the gentler approach,' she said to him. He was about to answer her but did not want to lose his opportunity with the man. 'You dirty foreign git,' he shouted after him.

By this time the man had reached Simone who offered him a leaflet. She looked lovely to Sorcha, in a white rumpled shirt, loose at the waist and tucked into her tight denims. Her runners gleamed, her hair shone and bounced in its ribbon. She smiled, her charm at full strength, and spoke to him. The man took the leaflet and stopped. He looked at it, looked at Simone and very earnestly asked her what it was about. They spoke for a few minutes, Simone swaying close to the man. Finally he went over to Paul who offered the petition to him. He signed and went on. Simone rushed over to see his address. She already had his name. Paul said, 'Sim, back off. He's too old. He's grown up, probably got kids, even your age.'

'I suppose,' she said, reluctantly. 'Well, I got him to sign.'

Clipboard had been watching the whole episode and was annoyed at Simone's success and his own failure. He came over. 'That's the last straw. You lot have half a minute to be gone. Out of here.'

'What's the problem now?' asked Paul, exasperated.

'She's stealing my business.' He walked over to Paul and shoved him hard against the wall of the GPO. 'Now get the hell out of here.' His face was centimetres from Paul's.

Sorcha did not know what to do. She was afraid of this man but didn't want to be intimidated. She felt that Roger would not be. She didn't have to wonder about that for long because Roger arrived just then, with Pam trailing behind him. He asked Sorcha what was happening and immediately walked over to clipboard.

People were taking notice at this stage. Sorcha was afraid a Garda would come along and that they'd all be in trouble. Roger put his hand on clipboard's shoulder. Clipboard pulled away but Roger gripped him very hard. He leaned towards him and spoke rapidly. None of them could hear much of what he said but clipboard turned around and walked back to his partner. They both moved off to the corner of Abbey Street, well out of the gang's way. 'Time for coffee,' called Roger, and they went across the road to the Kylemore Café, where the others were waiting.

Sorcha was thinking, as they dodged the cars, that Roger had looked very different just then. She tried to find a word for it, and sinister was the best she could do. She also found it intriguing that he handled clipboard so decisively, whatever he had said to him.

11

Summer moved along so stealthily that it was the middle of July
before anyone seemed to notice. When there was no school, time
was not sectioned off into small units that counted the days away.
The long, long days and short nights were distinguishable from
each other only by where they went or what they did. The days
of the week, even the hour of the day mattered little to them. Life
swirled comfortably past as the fresh newness imperceptibly left
the leaves, as flowers on the fruit trees faded and were replaced
by the tiny hard spheres and bulbs which gradually took on the
shape, and later the texture, of fruit.

The weather had held up for most of the time. People were
talking about a brilliant summer. So many years were dull and
misty and this year it was, for once, the real thing. This was a
summer in the way that summer should be. It got to the stage
where people woke up in the mornings with birdsong in their
ears and didn't even wonder about the weather. They forgot to
ask the daily question - 'What sort of a day is it?' - and instead
pulled their curtains to allow the waves of sunlight, loud almost
in its brightness, to wash over them. People didn't mind getting
up. There was good humour in the city. Clothes were light and
airy. Strangers smiled at each other. Of course there were the
grumblers, as the heat lay unmoving over the streets and the
fumes from the traffic were hot and heavy. Increasingly the cries
went up, 'It's shocking hot.' 'The heat'd kill you.' When the

weather finally broke, as it would inevitably, and the damp coolness that was much more typical of an Irish summer returned, the same people would lament the lack of sun and pine for Mediterranean coasts.

Paul and Sorcha were both tanned and felt healthy and good. Sometimes they walked to Three Rock and looked over the city, eating sandwiches, or sweets bought along the way. They were never alone there in those days. There were always noisy families and plenty of other picnickers to ensure that privacy was difficult to get. They often tried to find a quiet place where they could lie down together and enjoy the sun. Then they would kiss and cuddle each other. Sorcha enjoyed those days out and enjoyed Paul's company, but found that her mind was often on Roger and the group and all the issues that were involved. Paul was usually interested in talking about it and agreed, as they looked over the bay and the city from the mountain, or swam in the obviously polluted sea, that things were not good and that it was right that action be taken. But she often found that he would lose interest quite quickly and change the subject.

He wanted to talk about them, about her and him, and Sorcha often did not. Still, she sensed that she had to go along with him or there was not much point in the relationship. Besides, she enjoyed it when he told her how much she meant to him. Once he told her, that even though he was young, he thought that he loved her. This was when they were relaxed, not kissing or anything, and Sorcha felt very touched. She knew that Paul meant it seriously. She kissed him then, for a long time and grew very excited. That worried her too. She became afraid of what might happen, of what Paul might expect, of what she might expect herself.

Sorcha had been to other meetings with Roger and his group. Different people were at different sessions. Some of these she met only once, others seemed to be at all, or nearly all, of the meetings. She wondered were these some sort of core group, a special one? Several times things were said which seemed to hint at a private area, where she and others were not involved. Olivia,

Brenda, Eoin and George appeared regularly. So, of course, did Roger.

Different topics were discussed at these meetings. The most horrific was vivisection. George had explained how animals were used in experiments, often for no real scientific gain, only for profit. He showed slides one night and Sorcha was sickened by pictures of monkeys, still alive, with their skulls severed, cats and dogs with chemicals squirted in their eyes, mice and rats cut open while alive and all sorts of things inserted, animals dismembered or starved, or stuffed with food until they almost burst.

Sorcha always walked to and from the meetings with Roger. Mostly they talked of the issues or of some items on the news. Occasionally it was more personal.

'Look, Roger, I'm not saying that I don't like my parents or anything. I do. It's that sometimes, sometimes, they're so ...' Sorcha was saying on one such walk.

'I know. They're so much like parents, Sorcha. They don't want to let you grow up.' Roger said.

'Yes. That's it. It's not that they don't let me do things. I mean, they don't always treat me like a kid. They do take me seriously, let me do things. I can't explain it.'

'It's that they still feel responsible for you. Look, Sorcha, you're not a kid. My parents told me when I was sixteen that my life was my responsibility.'

'You know,' said Sorcha, 'you're right. It's my life. They don't see that. Not really.'

'Sorcha, everyone has to move away from their parents, to grow up. Sometimes that's painful, for both sides. It must be done, though.'

'But,' Sorcha was then a little distrustful of Roger, as she often was. She always felt that he was keeping something back. 'But you're still at home. You still live there.'

Roger laughed. 'Money, my child, money,' he said. He did not often joke, even in as small a way as that. 'Besides, I did move out, for a year. I lived in London in a house with some others. Two years ago. I learnt a lot there.'

Sorcha wondered what it had been like. Two years ago he would have been eighteen, only a little more than two years older than herself.

Sorcha's initial ban on tuna fish had been kept up, with no complaints from the family. After that she had insisted on free range eggs and for a while her parents objected because of the cost but Sorcha had explained to them how the hens were kept in cramped cages which kept them literally jammed up together all of their lives, never seeing daylight, with their beaks cut off to prevent them pecking each other to death. She told them that it was intolerable that humans should treat another species like that. She showed pictures and they agreed, so free range eggs it was. Everyone agreed that they were much nicer.

When she suggested recycling there was barely any objection at all. They were getting used to her. Nuala and Eoin (Sorcha at first thought it significant that one of the group had the same name as her father) often commented that it was better than having her drinking or drugtaking or dressing as a punk in Grafton Street. Sorcha could think of plenty of other things they would not like but said nothing about them.

So it was that the Raffertys got five separate bins. One held bottles, one cans, one papers. Each of these would be delivered for recycling. One held non-recyclable rubbish which was put out for collection. They had the smallest bin on the road each week, except for old Mrs O'Reilly who lived on her own four doors away. She hardly did anything, or used anything, she was so old. The fifth bin was for organic waste and this was the most controversial. Sorcha insisted on a compost heap in the back garden. No one in the family was a keen gardener and her parents did not want a smell. They fought but gave in on condition that Sorcha would plant vegetables only in a corner of the back garden and not put potatoes in the front, as she wanted to.

'You'll never look after any of these,' said Eoin as he watched her plant carrots and peas.

'Just you wait, know-all. I'm a changed person.'

'That's for sure,' said her father and gave her a playful tap on the head. 'Gone looney and impertinent in the one summer. What on earth next?'

* * *

One evening Sorcha was in the kitchen tidying up after dinner. The intense heat had left the day but it was still warm enough for tee shirt and shorts. The long summer twilight has begun and the blue grey evening was perfectly still. As she washed dishes she watched a pair of thrushes on the tree in the garden, one pecking at the net of nuts she had left hanging for them, the other singing, and to Sorcha it seemed as if they were calling in the day to put it to bed. As the sky darkened the birdsong would quieten until the birds slipped off for the few hours until daybreak. The sky in the West was streaked with cloud - red, purple, even greenish. The cat sat patiently on the wall, intent on the birds.

Sorcha was just waking from the pure pleasure of the scene to the thoughts of how chemicals, emissions of all sorts, pesticides were slowly clogging it all up, killing the insects, poisoning the birds, destroying the air and water, when her brother, Conor, burst into the kitchen.

'Hello, baby sister. How is the world? Will we survive to the new term?'

Sorcha turned and sprayed him with soapy water from the sink. She had hardly seen him all summer and was delighted that he was here now, even if he would give her a hard time.

'We might, big brother, we might. Just about. But we must be careful.'

'Why is that?'

'There are dark forces about, evil ones.'

'Ah, I see. Then it is true. You have gone daft. Dad said so.'

'What would he know? After all he sells suits all day.'

'Now, now be fair to him.'

'Conor, remember we used to call him stodgy?' said Sorcha, suddenly excited. She loved remembering with Conor. The family memories were so strong, went so far back.

Conor laughed. 'Yeh. To prove he wasn't, remember what he used to get up to.'

'The time he swung out of the rope ladder.'

'In the garden,' Conor remembered, excited now with Sorcha. 'And he slipped. His leg.'

'And his back. For days.'

Their father had fallen and become entangled in the home-made rope ladder, had hung almost upside down until they had rescued him. His embarrassment had been bad enough but it had been weeks before his wrenched back had stopped paining. They laughed at it again, with no need to describe it all. The incident had been recalled so often that the words were only pointers, reminders, keys to the shared memories. They released a few more stories and were warm and relaxed with each other as the colours left the streaks of cloud in the West and the sky blackened to the East side of the garden.

They went outside and Sorcha showed Conor her planting, shadows now, not clearly seen. They breathed in the heaviness of the night-scented stock, in full flower. Sorcha linked Conor's arm and asked him about college. He told her stories, some he'd told before, some new ones. She asked him about study, about what he would do after he finished.

Then Sorcha said, 'Conor, I don't think I'm interested in college any more.'

There was quite a long pause which Conor ended by saying, 'Why?' She could feel him forcing himself to be cool. The idea of either of them not going to college was almost beyond imagining.

She said, 'What's the point? I could study, say engineering, or law or anything. What good would it do? I'd get a job, become part of the scene. I'd contribute.'

'What do you mean, you'd contribute? To what?'

'To everything that leads to, you know, planetary destruction.' Sorcha had picked up some of the phrases from the group.

'Sorcha, don't be silly. The Green movement isn't a weirdo drop out movement any more. It's part of things. They need lawyers, scientists, everything, if that's what you're into.'

'Well, no. Look Conor, if you're not in this, you're against it. It's that simple.'

'What's this "it"? Is this a bloody religion? Who are these people you're involved with?'

'What do you know? What have you heard? Have they been talking to you?' Sorcha was suspicious of him now.

'Who?'

'Mom and Dad! Is that why you're here? To talk to poor Sorcha because we're all concerned about her?'

'They just asked me, if I was around, to ...'

'Stupid!' Suddenly Sorcha was flaming, angry, both with them for interfering and with Conor for agreeing. 'Stupid! Stupid! Stupid! They have to let go, to let me grow up. It's painful for both sides, you know, me and them. I have to be separate from them.' Again she used the language of Roger and the others.

They talked on, moving back into the house when it got cool. There was now only a suggestion of light on the city skyline, which wouldn't really go away before dawn came again. Sorcha calmed, and was able to talk to Conor again. He could see her point but was firm on the idea that she should go to college, then decide.

'Anyway it's two years away. And I know that this job,' he was referring to his summer job in a petrol station, 'or anything like it would kill you. You need to use your brains. You've buckets of the things.' Sorcha liked to be told that.

Conor took a can from the fridge, as he told Sorcha about his girlfriend, Sally. Sorcha had not yet met her and asked him to bring her over so that she could. A few times he remarked how mature Sorcha was, in her manner. She knew that if anyone else said that to her she would be angry, but Conor was so un-condescending that it was a genuine compliment. She talked about Paul and tried to tell him some of the doubts she had about being so serious about one boy at her age. She wasn't sure that

Paul was the right person for her anyway. Conor could understand why she was uneasy but said that if she really loved Paul she shouldn't worry. He said that this wasn't the sort of thing that could be worked out to a master plan and that she had to follow her feelings.

As their talk wound down, Conor, stretching, sleepily said, 'Well, Sorcha, It's good to have a chat. I hardly ever see you, so I suppose we gorge ourselves when we do meet.'

'It's fun to be a glutton, sometimes.'

Sorcha picked up her book, ready to go to bed. The earlier upset had been forgotten. She was surprised at what happened next and even though she thought about it afterwards, she couldn't really make sense of what she did. Roger was not much help when she asked him about it. He just told her that she had done her duty, what she had to do, that even family must be made see the light. Paul was appalled and refused to support her at all.

Conor finished his drink and threw his can into the bin - into the organic waste bin for the compost heap. Sorcha turned to him, disbelief making her wordless for a few seconds.

Then she said, icily, 'Look at what you've done.' Conor didn't know what she was talking about. 'The can,' she said, icier.

'Oh. The garden will die. The can will stop the biological and chemical breakdown of the organic matter.'

'Take it out,' she said.

'Hold on until I remove these rotting potato skins. Here's some slimy carrot peelings. And a little bit of soggy tea leaves. Lovely.' Conor mimed rooting in the bin but did not touch anything.

Sorcha exploded, the ice shattering in a flaming ball of anger and unreason. 'You stupid moron. You silly, shallow twit. You study science. You see nothing. You and your creeping, toadying, slimeball, moneygrabbing animal murderers don't care. You fill the world with your crap and deny there's any problem and then deny that it's your self-centred greed that caused it when you at last can't deny the facts any more.' She shouted on and on and Conor tried to stop her. She finally hit him and screamed, 'I hate you. I really do.'

He turned and walked out of the kitchen, out of the house. It was only later that she could see the hurt she had caused, and then she couldn't explain why she had done it.

Her father came down to see why there was so much noise. 'Having a row?' he asked, as light-heartedly as possible.

Sorcha recognised the strategy. Avoid antagonising her, then tell her what's what. 'I hate you too. More than him,' she screamed and scorched to her room where she cried far into the night, unable to calm the storm howling and tearing inside her.

At one stage during the night she had a visit from the Smiths, all four of them. They were beginning to irritate her. She found that when a fantasy as detailed and consistent as the Smiths had been around for such a long time it was difficult not to refer to them in hard times. For Sorcha this night was certainly a hard time. Mrs Smith came sidling into the room, Alice Smith a few paces behind her. 'Now, Sorcha,' said Mrs Smith, 'this really is a dreadful situation. It really is. I was just saying to Mr Smith, wasn't I, Alice? that this is a dreadful situation.' Alice nodded, wide-eyed, respectful confirmation. Mr Smith appeared in slippers, slacks and cardigan, his casual wear. 'Yes, a dreadful situation. We were just saying it. All this recycling is rubbish. Rubbish. It won't do.' 'I agree,' chimed Mrs Smith, 'we'll all be out of work, nothing to make. Dreadful.' 'Dreadful,' agreed Mr Smith, 'Don't you agree, Alice?' 'Yes, Daddy,' cooed Alice, her hands clasped in front of her midriff. Simon Smith stayed in the background, his usual smirk gone, looking for once as if he was fully behind the others.

'Oh, go away, you silly stupid morons,' Sorcha barked at them. They faded, even before she had the first word exploding through her teeth. She found no comfort in the stupidity of the Smiths. Stupidity in the world had become a worry to her, something that was driving her more and more to want to change the way things were, no longer a reason to feel smug and superior, no longer something to laugh at.

12

Paul and Pam were out walking. They felt, each of them, a little uncomfortable. The back of Paul's throat was taut from tension and Pam's palms were dampish. They had known each other for a long time but had never spent more than a few minutes alone together. Earlier in the evening Pam had called for Sorcha but she had been out. Pam had talked to Nuala and Eoin for half an hour or so and then left. Paul was arriving.

'No good going in there. She's at a meeting,' said Pam to him.

'Oh. I didn't know she was going. Was she with Roger?' asked Paul.

'I don't know. I didn't see her. Her mum and dad told me.'

'She's hard to find these days, isn't she?' said Paul.

'Yeh. Always at something or other. No one else around either.'

'No. Might as well go home myself. See you, Pam.'

'Yeh, see you, Paul.'

They turned to go their separate ways and had walked only a few steps when Pam turned. Paul had stopped and was turning back.

'Want to go for a walk?' she asked.

'Why not? Better than staying in on a night like this.' The evening was warm and slowly fading to night.

'Yeh. There's nothing on telly anyway,' said Pam.

'You know, I've hardly watched telly for weeks,' Paul said.

'Sign of a good summer,' said Pam.

They walked in silence for a while, suddenly becoming aware of each other and of the silence. The usual distractions, the gang and the joking were gone and they had to talk directly to each other. It was never as easy to tease when there were just two people.

'Have you seen Jeff lately?' Pam ventured, 'he's gone daft on that girl from Marino. What's her name, Jenny.'

'Yeh, I've hardly seen him for weeks. He's even crazier than usual.'

'That would be hard,' said Pam, laughing, forcing it a little. 'Simone will give him plenty of advice, anyway.'

'Poor old Sim,' said Paul. 'She's harmless. I just hope she doesn't end up pregnant some day.'

'Oh, she's not at it, not like that,' said Pam quickly.

'How do you know?' asked Paul.

Pam felt that this topic was OK for joking with the gang or for talking to Sorcha about but could be a bit too much for just the two of them. She was curious also to hear what Paul knew about Simone and how he knew it but decided it was safer to get off the subject.

'Remember the first day we gave out the leaflets. You got into some sort of fight over her.'

'Hey come on, it wasn't over her. It was that creep with clipboard. Creep with Clipboard. Sounds good.'

'Roger had to sort him out for you,' teased Pam. Paul's reaction was all right. He wasn't annoyed so they could continue on their course, Simone safely out of the way.

'Yeh, he's tough, in funny way, Roger,' said Paul.

'You know, I never thought of him like that. Always imagined him as a quiet, dreamy sort.'

'Fancy him, do you?'

'Get lost. Fancy him? He's weird.'

'I agree. Sorcha seems to like him, though.'

Pam supposed Paul was jealous. She would have been, in his situation. Paul was wondering whether Pam knew anything about Sorcha and Roger. Maybe they talked, girl talk. He decided to ask her, straight out.

'Does she ever talk about him, Sorcha about Roger, I mean?'

'Oh, a bit, you know.' Pam didn't want to give anything away that she shouldn't. 'Sorcha's changed. Have you noticed?'

'How exactly?' asked Paul.

'Well, she's really into this thing. It's not just conservation, recycling and stuff. That's OK. We all agree with that, no problem. It's an alternative lifestyle, though, for her. She won't use buses any more.'

'I can see her point, they're so bad.'

'Ha, ha.' Pam responded to his bad joke in the usual way. 'But that's not the point. She actually thinks everyone should only walk or cycle.'

'I know. It's kind of over the top. All of a sudden, she doesn't want to go anywhere further than walking distance. All our trips to the sea are in danger. Maybe we'll get horses. High-ho, Silver, away.' Paul mimed the Lone Ranger for a moment or two. Pam laughed and they were both relaxed, suddenly. Their discomfort had been lessening as they talked, and it disappeared with the joke.

Pam went on, 'She's given up all junk food as well. She won't eat sweets, drink minerals or anything like that. Organic vegetables, free range eggs. Bet she'll go veggie soon.'

'She's been talking about it all right. Did she show you what she's planted. They're doing OK too. Rabbit food.'

Pam gripped her bottom lip with her upper teeth and began a remarkably good imitation of Bugs Bunny. 'Eh, what's up, Doc? What's this recycling busy-ness all about, eh?'

They were walking close together and Paul swung his hip, hitting Pam and knocking her off her stride. She stumbled and turned and swiped at him. He dodged and, laughing, they walked on.

'Does she talk about Roger much?' Paul tried again.

'Never talks about anything else. Not him, I mean but the whole thing, these meetings, the Corpo's road plans, pollution, whales. You name it.'

'Yeh. It's kind of the same with me. Not all the time though. I wonder what's happening. Where will it all go?'

'Sorcha, you mean?'

'Sorcha and me. I'm serious about her, Pam, but she's drifting away.'

As he said this they were both uncomfortable again. It was as if they could not talk about Paul's feeling for Sorcha while they were joking and enjoying themselves. They both wondered about this, privately. Did it mean that they were becoming attracted to each other? Did that mean they were being unfair to Sorcha, betraying her? What did their being friends mean?

'Look, Paul, Sorcha is mad about you. That's definite. Roger is more of ...' Pam tried to find the words. She had decided that she had to be loyal to Sorcha. She herself might be friends with Paul, but that was as far as she was going to go. Sorcha and Paul were a couple, she wasn't going to butt in by giving Paul the impression that he was losing ground with Sorcha. 'Roger is more of a fascination for her. That's it. You know the way that snakes kind of hypnotise their prey. Mesmerise it. Sorcha's sort of mesmerised.'

'Is he going to strike? That's what the snakes do, isn't it? Is he a snake? Is that what you're saying?'

'I don't know, Paul. Roger is different. He's dangerous. I don't trust him. Remember what we were talking about, the leaflets.'

'Creep with Clipboard.'

'He wasn't like us then. He scared Creep with Clipboard in two seconds. I found that scary. I hope she's not getting into something she shouldn't.'

'So do I. What'll we do?'

Pam could not resist it. 'We'll have to console each other, won't we?' She leaned against him for a moment and he quickly put his arm around her shoulders and then took it away.

They chatted about other things until they reached the end of their walk. Once again they were both uncomfortable, unsure of how to end the evening. Should they acknowledge that they had changed with each other, as they certainly had, after talking so much on their own. To do so, to kiss briefly say, would be to say that they wanted things to go on like that, to develop into something more. To simply say goodbye would be to leave it all open to whatever happened next. Of course they could have said, 'Hey, let's take it easy, ease off,' but neither wanted to do that. Neither of them was sure what the other wanted and neither was prepared to say something that would seem foolish. What if the other hadn't even noticed anything to hold off from? Whoever spoke first risked being left out on a limb, feeling silly. In the end it was caution, self protection, that decided each of them to take the middle way. The thoughts that rushed through each of their minds as they stood on the corner near Paul's house were remarkably similar.

They looked at each other, right in the eyes. After a pause, how meaningful or significant neither could be sure, Paul broke the silence, 'Yeh, Pam. See you later.'

They went home, darkness all but complete, the street lights strengthening against the pale streaks of daylight over the roof-tops.

13

It was Sunday afternoon, the last in July. The weather, as if by a miracle, had held up. There had been a few cloudy days, but these had been hot and sultry, thundery days although the thunder held off. Occasionally a faint rumble was heard in the distance, like a predatory beast making sure it was not forgotten. It was the sort of weather that makes people uneasy. Then it had brightened again. People were talking about the greenhouse effect and the hole in the ozone layer being responsible. A local joke was that if this was the greenhouse effect we should have had pollution years ago. Sorcha was irritated by this attitude. It showed, again, that people didn't take the catastrophe that was surely coming seriously.

Eoin and Nuala had driven to the country for the afternoon to visit friends and Sorcha had not wanted to go with them. Everyone else had disappeared as well. Sorcha didn't mind: she was finding the gang more and more difficult to be with. Their endless slagging, the lack of seriousness about serious things, was irritating her more and more. She preferred to see only Pam and Paul. She phoned Paul and asked him to come over. They lay out in the back garden in the sun, relaxed and barely talking, holding hands comfortably. After a while it got too warm so they went inside. Paul went to the fridge and found a can of Coke. Sorcha poured a glass of water from the filter jug she kept beside the sink. She couldn't bear the idea of drinking the chemicals they put in the water supply.

Paul noticed this and said, 'Hey, what's that yoke? A flask? Hidden booze?'

'A filter. It extracts all the gunge they put in.'

'I thought all that stuff, the fluoride, was good for you?'

'So they say. It's good for your teeth OK, but what about side effects? Anyway there's chlorine and aluminium as well, to mention just the nice ones.'

'Yeh, but no bugs. Not a germ, not even a teeny weeny one to be found leaping around in the tap. Healthy, no?'

'Maybe. Maybe not. You have to weigh it up. You see, Paul, some bacteria might be ...'

'Ha, I see. Use the head,' Paul interrupted, not wanting another long discussion on environmental issues. 'Come here and kiss me. It's a perfect day for it and there's no one around to disturb us. We could do anything.'

Sorcha was not able to get into Paul's mood quite that quickly. She was still thinking about the water. 'It's trying to get the balance right. I really don't know, Paul, what's the best.' She had paid no attention to Paul and his kiss. He was hurt.

'Look, Sorcha, this is getting to be too much. Do you never think of anything else any more?'

'Of course I do. But if we don't get all of this right soon we won't be able to think at all.'

'Look, you're right. I'm not trying to stop you,' Paul began and Sorcha said, in interruption, 'You'd better not be,' but he went on, ignoring her, 'I'm as interested as you. I want to be involved, you know. I'd like to go to some of your meetings.'

'You know you have to be invited,' Sorcha said quickly, not wanting to put him off.

'So you keep telling me. Look, Sorcha, if all you ever do, or say, or think about is ozone layers, nuclear holocausts, mink farms, endangered teddy bears and so on, it gets so boring. We'd be better off with no planet. I can see life in the future. Caves, raw roots. No thanks. There must be another way.'

Sorcha was quiet. She knew that Paul was not as interested as her. She liked him. She wanted to be with him and would have loved it if he thought like her. But to him this was all an extra, more like a hobby. Sorcha knew that she could not take it or leave it according to her mood. It was no good drinking filtered water today and junky minerals tomorrow, no good worrying about rain forests and eating burgers in fast food places. She could probably have persuaded Roger to invite Paul to one of the meetings but she was afraid that he might make a fool of himself. She knew that Roger did not think much of Paul, anyway.

She walked over to him, put her arms around his waist and kissed him on the mouth. Paul kissed her back but soon stopped. He felt that it was important to try to sort out what was going on, what they were going to do.

He said, 'Look, Sorcha, Pam agrees. You really are going over the top in all this.'

Sorcha was annoyed that Pam had been talking to Paul. 'What's this? Talking behind my back. What are you two up to?' She could feel herself getting angry. She didn't want another session like the one with Conor. She controlled herself.

'Hey, Pam.' Paul stopped. Why had he called her Pam? 'I mean Sorcha,' he changed quickly, 'there's nothing. We've just chatted a few times. You weren't around. Meetings.' Paul was flustered.

Sorcha felt a sudden pang inside, and all of a sudden she was jealous. She had never really felt jealousy of this sort before. The effect was confusing. She was scared that Paul would go off and yet she didn't want to make a fool of herself by saying anything. She didn't own him, after all. 'You don't have to explain. You're entitled to talk to who you like. You don't need my permission. I don't own you. You don't own me.'

'Look, Sorcha, you're important to me. You really are. You know that. I just think that maybe I'm not important to you, not any more. That's all.'

'You are. Of course you are,' Sorcha said quickly. The thought that she was hurting Paul was upsetting her, yet even as she said it she felt the doubt rumbling in the background. She wondered how she could be jealous, if at the same time she was so unsure about him. At least at the meetings feelings were a lot simpler, she thought.

'Do you mean it? Really?' He looked at her. Like a dog, wide-eyed and pleading, thought Sorcha and fought to put irreverent ideas out of her mind.

'Yes, Paul, yes,' she said, feelings for him, to her relief, washing over her. She kissed him again, this time wanting to. He responded, clutching her to him, holding her tight, glad that it seemed OK again. After a while, she said, 'I love you,' sure of it then.

They started talking again. They both found that the kissing had made them feel warm towards each other. But still Paul wanted to sort everything out. Right then, he felt that he and Sorcha were good together, that they meant a lot to each other. He was still slow to say 'love', although Sorcha had said it often enough to him. He knew, though, that feeling good now was not enough. Later on, after he had gone home, or the next day, the doubts would start again. He would begin, again, to ask where did he fit in to Sorcha's life. He knew that he would wonder about Roger and what his place was in Sorcha's life.

'Tell me about Roger. Out straight. Are you going with him?'

'Paul! I'm not, not, not. How many times do I have to tell you. Roger is part of this group. There are others there as well. He means nothing to me, apart from that. That's all. I'm not giving up the group. You can like that, or lump it.'

'I'm not asking you to, I think. But, look, I'll just have to take your word about Roger. I'm just jealous, that's all.'

'I suppose I'm lucky, you being jealous.' Sorcha said nothing about her feelings about him and Pam.

'I don't want to get caught up in all this serious stuff. We're too young. Sorcha, I've got to get on with life. Capital letters LIFE. Let the oldies get dried up and serious.'

'That's the problem. What do you mean by "capital letters LIFE"?'

Paul said, 'I mean, having fun. Doing what I want to do. Being myself. Finding out things. Music, reading, you.'

'Sure. I want all that too. But there's more. On its own that's so shallow, so pointless.'

'No, it's not. We're young, I keep telling you. When we're old and soggy and stodgy and thirty-seven then we can look after the world.'

'That, as you know, is what's wrong. Everyone now knows that there's a problem. Leave it to someone else. I don't want to be like that, Paul.'

'What do you want to be like? Who? Roger? He's a dried up prune. He's like an aul' fella at twenty.'

'That's not fair. Just because you don't like him. You hardly know him anyway. You only met him a few times. He's serious, I know, hard to get to know. He's honest though. And he doesn't have to slag all the time. He's not afraid of his feelings. He's not afraid to be serious. About things.'

'About you, I suppose.'

'Shut up. I told you.' Sorcha said, playfully enough. She began to see very clearly, with a sinking feeling, that what she was doing with Roger and his group was having an effect on her, or at least on everyone around her. If she continued as she was she would eventually put Paul off. Her parents, she knew, were having problems with her as well. They too said she was changing. But surely changing was part of life. She couldn't be a kid forever. Roger had said that and he was right. And if she was changing, and Paul was not, they would eventually have nothing in common. Then they would finish up. She didn't want that. It was nice to have a boyfriend, to be with someone. It made her feel good, secure. She liked the fact that she knew that Paul cared for her in a special way. She liked the way she could actually touch him, feel him and be comfortable about it.

So, she could drop her other activities, become normal. That was what it was all about. She could behave like everyone else, speak about the terrible state of the planet now and again, in front of the telly munching sweets, and get on with life in capital letters. What would she turn out to be then? She didn't know, but felt that it was not what she wanted to be. Paul and the others, Pam as well, were happy just going along, having fun, ignoring anything serious. Roger had said to her that an unexamined life is not worth living - he said Socrates had said that thousands of years ago. Why did they not learn that in school, she wondered? It might make people think. But then, she knew, most people didn't want to think. That was why Paul thought she wasn't normal any more.

'I suppose,' Sorcha began.

Paul waited. Then he said, 'Interesting. I suppose we all suppose. At least I suppose we're supposed to suppose from time to time. Supposing, supposing three bears were ...'

'Shut up. Again. I suppose I'll cut back on the group and meetings. I'll be normal.'

'Aw, Sorcha. Of course you're normal. Sort of, anyway.'

Paul was slagging again, and she enjoyed that. She twisted her face and contorted her body and hobbled across the room. 'I'll be normal from now on, I promise, my master.'

As Paul was leaving, the Smiths hovered into view. Sorcha looked at them as they prepared to comment. She got there before them. 'Your day has come, Smiths. I have to look after myself from now on. I'm a big girl. I have to look to the consequences of things. Bye.' A missile, laser controlled, swooped in from the sky and the Smiths, Mr, Mrs, Alice and Simon were vaporised in the flash.

14

The next evening Sorcha called to Roger's house. He answered the door.

'Sorcha, I'm quite surprised to see you. There's no meeting tonight.'

'I know that, Roger. I wanted to talk. Can I come in?'

Roger didn't reply immediately. He looked straight into Sorcha's eyes, unwavering. As always, Sorcha was forced to think when he did this, to be fully aware of her own feelings. He didn't stand aside either and she began to feel embarrassed, wishing she had not come. What had given her the idea that he would want to see her unexpectedly like this when there was no meeting to go to? Finally he seemed to decide and said, 'It's not a good time to come in right now, but I could walk with you for ten minutes. Would that be all right?'

Sorcha wanted to tell him to get lost, to say that if he didn't want to talk to her to forget about it but she said, 'That'd be great, Roger.'

'Wait here,' he said and went inside, shutting the door. Now Sorcha really was annoyed and wanted to bang on the door and leave but she did what he said and waited. She wondered whether he had a girl inside. After three minutes which seemed like an hour, during which Sorcha heard a voice raised inside the house, he came back and said, 'Well, come on then,' and walked down the garden. He seemed irritated. She followed quickly.

As they walked along the street under the heavy August leaves and the ripening chestnuts, Roger looked at his watch. Sorcha knew that ten minutes would be just that, not fifteen, nor even twelve.

'Roger,' she began, not wanting to waste time but having to fight away nervousness. 'I want your advice.' Of course, he said nothing, looked at her, left it up to her to go on or not. 'I don't know where my life is going. It seems that if I go on like this, with the group, with you and so on, that I'll lose everything. Paul is drifting away from me. Even my parents. I'm torn, Roger. I have to decide what sort of life I want.'

'That's exactly it, Sorcha. You have to decide. No one else can do it for you. This world is rotten, Sorcha. Don't forget that. Not the planet, not nature, things as they were intended, but us, human society is. You know that. They conspire to take, to abuse, to destroy and lay waste for short term gain. There is no collective responsibility, only individuals indulging themselves. The driving idea is to be selfishly yourself, to do as you see fit. Being truly yourself, with commitment, concern for the future, for the common good, has no place for people anymore. For us to survive we must be disciplined. We must be answerable to the rest of the community. To the group. To the planet. Otherwise we will go down, the whole race will, like the Titanic in the ocean. There will be no survivors, though.' He paused, still searching her with his eyes. 'Go on,' said Sorcha, familiar by now with what he was saying.

'Relationships, the way they are conducted by most people, are selfish. People should get together to bring children into the world and to educate and train their children. Now, like everything else, it's sentimental and self indulgent. There is no responsibility. So we have crime, assault, rape. We must put things right, or there will be no future. To do so we must make sacrifices. These will be personal and communal.'

Roger was going further than he ever had before and Sorcha could feel his eyes boring into her, willing her to accept what he was saying.

'So, you see, you have to decide. I can't do it for you. Which life do you want? Education, a career, every comfort for you and your children and ultimately, unhappiness and destruction for the whole world. Or to fight, to be in the vanguard, to take a stand, difficult though it is. To be full of courage and hope. It's your decision, Sorcha. No one else's.'

Roger had guided them on a walk that was bringing them back to his house. He looked at his watch. The ten minutes were nearly up.

Sorcha did not know what to do. Put like this, there seemed to be no option. He sounded so right. She supposed she had wanted Roger to decide for her, not to leave it up to her. They were at his gate. 'Well,' he said, 'you don't have to decide now, this minute, you know.' He was gentler for a moment, aware of her turmoil.

'Oh, I think I do,' she said and reached up to kiss him. Half to her surprise he responded by taking her face in his hands and kissing her full on the lips. It was so confident, so definite, his lips were so firm and so sure that she was startled. 'OK. Fine,' he said and turned and went in.

It was only on the way home that she thought of the proper word for Roger's kiss. Cold. Was she crazy, deciding for that? But no, it was for a life, not for a person, she was deciding.

So this is it, she said to herself, when she got home. She was in her room looking at herself in the mirror. She adjusted her hair a few times but soon lost interest in doing that. It didn't seem appropriate. Sorcha had decided that she could not be content with herself if she lived like the others. She hoped that she could continue as she was, become even more involved in the activities of the group and still have her friends and her family. She was frightened, deep down, that this would not be possible. She had told Roger as much, and knew that this was not important to him. But it was to her. What would she do if they finally got tired of her, if her parents threw her out for being crazy or weird? She knew that no matter how she felt, it was most likely that she and Paul would break up someday, anyway. That was obviously what happened to most people of her age going out with each other. She hated the idea though, and wondered, like most people her age, if it could go on forever. 'Not if I continue as I am, anyway,' she said out loud and made a face at herself in the mirror.

Then she thought of kissing Roger. Why would she want to do that if she was with Paul? That didn't seem to tie in. She felt if you were with one person that was it, there was no room for someone else. Yet she knew that she wasn't fully happy with Paul. She often felt unhappy about some aspect of their relationship, or with him or his behaviour. But that had never meant that she wanted to kiss anyone else.

And why did Roger kiss her back? He was quite capable of putting her down, if he had wanted to, of telling her not to be silly. He had only given her ten minutes of his precious time anyway. If he was mad about her he would have made more effort, have shown her that he was. So, she wondered, was he using her? She had accused Paul of that before without really meaning it. With Roger it was different. She could really believe that he would use her, in any way that suited him. She remembered handing out the leaflets. She hadn't been happy when he hadn't treated her or the others with proper seriousness and respect. But he had said that she was different, had seemed to respect her. Again she spoke aloud. 'This is all too complicated for you, Sorcha.'

And then there was the coldness of his kiss. She couldn't decide if he kissed her back because he wanted to or because he was trying to persuade her to decide for him and the group. She certainly had not felt any passion, or concern, or love that she felt when kissing Paul. But it was exciting, in a strange sort of way. She suddenly realised that it had felt like a dangerous thing to do. Dangerous, because it was like a sign that she was getting involved in something very serious and might expect anything to happen. Or might be expected to do anything, for the cause.

15

Paul had been upset since being with Sorcha on Sunday, as he knew he would be. He spent all day Monday thinking about it. Monday was his day off from the shop where he was working for the summer. He stayed in bed late and only got up when his mother threatened to go on strike if he didn't get himself and his laziness down to the shops and get the messages. He decided that he was miserable enough without having to listen to her ranting as well and at least going to the shops would get him out of the house for a few minutes. He dressed, without washing, in the same clothes he had worn the day before.

'What do you want, O Great Mother?'

'Ha! Talking like that will get you nowhere. Not when you come down at half past twelve. Here's a list.'

'Ah, a list. Let me see now. Three large bottles of orange, a six-bag of crisps, ten bars of chocolate, chips.'

'Shut up, Paul and go to the shops. Did you wash your hair this week?'

'Yes, darling Mother, on Tuesday.'

'This is Monday. That's a week. Do it today.'

'Or else what?' he said, trying to make her crosser.

'No or else. Just do it. Now get out.'

When Paul left his mother was talking darkly to herself about the dangers of too much education and how she should have sent him out to work after his Inter. He slumped the moment he was out on the street. He kept a look out for Sorcha as he went to the shops but there was no sign. He desperately wanted to meet her but he knew that meeting would not be enough. He also wanted some sign, some sign from her that would tell him that everything was all right between them. Like Sorcha, Paul knew enough to realise that few people of their age went on forever. Yet he believed that his and Sorcha's relationship was special. They could talk about almost anything. They really enjoyed each other's company. She was good fun, or had been until recently. She was sexy too. He enjoyed that but Paul was not like some of his friends, the others he knew. All they seemed interested in was the sex side of going out with girls. Paul enjoyed kissing Sorcha but he never wanted things to get out of control. Sometimes he was afraid that she might not have enough sense but he was much happier keeping things as they were. He considered Sorcha to be his friend as well as his girlfriend.

After the first evening that he had walked with Pam they had met again by accident a few times. Paul had enjoyed their walks and had begun to hope that there would be more of them. It was not as if he fancied Pam. Not really. But he did like her quite a lot. Not in the way he liked Sorcha. He supposed that was love but did not like to use that word too easily. Pam, though, was much more relaxed than Sorcha at the moment. She was not as bright as Sorcha, nor as witty when they were slagging. The thing was, though, that she wasn't so serious either. Sorcha was, more and more, interested in one thing, the environment. Pam was more like anyone else, a bit of crack, a bit of gossip, jokes and so on. He also thought that she was very attractive, really nice. He had never particularly noticed that about her before. He wondered what it would be like to kiss her, to hold her. When they were messing, walking along those evenings, he had put his arm around her a few times and she had put hers around him. He thought she felt nice then.

Paul felt quite guilty about all of this. On the one hand it didn't seem fair that he was beginning to fancy Pam when he was so serious about Sorcha. On the other hand Sorcha was Pam's best friend, so it was worse than if it had been someone else. Then again, Paul felt that maybe it was time to take up with someone else, even if it wasn't Pam, and finish with Sorcha. But if that was so, why did he feel so worried about Sorcha, and why did he want to see her, and to make it all right with her? 'This is too complicated for you, Paul,' he said aloud.

He got the shopping and brought it home. He told his mother that he was going for a walk and walked for a long while, his thoughts filling his head, wondering why he was miserable when being in love (if that is what it was) was supposed to make you happy.

He only noticed where he was when he got to North Frederick Street and decided to continue on the short distance into town and see what was happening. The holiday season had begun and it was relatively quiet, otherwise he might not have noticed Creep with Clipboard outside Clerys. The Creep became a sudden symbol of all Paul's problems. He had been there the day Roger had had to rescue them, and Paul had to admit to himself, if not to anyone else, that he had been at a loss until Roger had come along. Roger had had little private words with Sorcha a few times that day. Pam had slagged him about the incident several times. Without too much thinking or planning Paul walked past the line seller, turned around and came back. He had half decided on what to do if the Creep approached him. If he didn't, he would probably walk by. There was no need to walk by.

'Excuse me, can I talk to you for a minute? It won't take long.' The clipboard was held down, not too obviously in view. Paul stopped. Clipboard stopped. Paul looked him straight in the eye and held it. At first Clipboard didn't notice. 'Thank you, Sir,' he began.

Paul interrupted, 'Don't call me Sir. I'm younger that you, you miserable self-centered twit. Take your puny little body and that silly clipboard and put both of them in some stinking hell hole somewhere far from here.' Paul looked with satisfaction at the boy's lower jaw as it dropped, as if a restraining cord had been cut, or a catch loosened. 'Need I go on?' he asked and stepped out onto the road, dodging neatly in and out of the traffic and trying to do so without seeming to hurry.

Paul's heart was pounding with excitement. He was almost dizzy. He could hardly believe that he had said that to a live person, in all seriousness. He had been practising insults in his room for months and had no chance to use them in a real situation until then. He was delighted with his performance. He had managed to insert 'clipboard' into the place he had left available for the most suitable word for the occasion when rehearsing the tirade. He hadn't even paused. And his opening, although unrehearsed, had been perfect. He supposed that practice gave one confidence, gave one the courage to improvise.

He was at the top of Eason's steps when he noticed another clipboard. He stopped to look at him and his heart gave an extra thump. This one looked much more like the original than the one across the street, no doubt still stunned from his encounter with Paul, who had appeared out of nowhere and disappeared into the traffic. Paul was blushing terribly and sweating profusely as he pushed open the door of the shop and slipped past the security guard and his chattering radio.

16

Sorcha decided to give up trying to figure everything out and went down to watch TV. Her mother and father were in the room. Her mother picked up the remote control and switched off the set when Sorcha walked in.

'Must have been a good one,' she said as she flopped into one of the easy chairs, slouching way down. She constantly claimed that she never got to watch good programmes because Eoin and Nuala, the united front, said they were unsuitable.

'It's not the telly. We want to talk to you,' her father said.

'Oh,' said Sorcha, quickly checking mentally what she might have done wrong. She figured that it was serious because of their attitude and because he had said 'we', not 'I'. They had been discussing this beforehand. Her usual strategy was to say nothing at the start, until she knew what was going on. Then she could decide to argue or to shut up, depending on her own mood and the seriousness of the subject.

'Sit up straight, will you, that's bad for your back,' said her mother. That did not sound good. Sorcha sat up.

'Sorcha, we're both concerned about you,' said her father. Sorcha relaxed a little. It was only going to be general stuff, she hoped. That was never so bad. It usually ended in a reasonably civilised discussion, not a row, or new rules or anything. She said nothing.

'Yes,' said her mother. 'Lately you've been different. Difficult to get on with.'

'Ah, mother, give us a break,' Sorcha burst out, against her intention to stay cool.

'This is an example of what we mean,' said her father. 'Every time anyone speaks to you, you snap at them.'

'And all the demands you've been making, recycling and so on,' said her mother.

'But you agreed that they're good,' said Sorcha, alarmed at the idea of an attack on what she now considered vital principles.

'Yes, we did. But there is a limit. You've gone beyond it in everything, not just recycling,' said her father.

They're taking turns, thought Sorcha.

'Look, Sorcha, that's not the real issue here,' said her mother.

'What is it then?' asked Sorcha, deciding to try to get it over with as soon as possible.

'We're worried about these meetings you go to, and this boy Roger. We don't know who these people are. They're so much older than you,' said her father.

'I told you before. They're Olivia and Brenda and ... '

'Don't get cheeky. We don't know anything about them, about their families, what they're doing.' It was her mother's turn.

Sorcha started to laugh. 'What's funny?' said her father, getting cross.

'You two. You're like Zig and Zag, taking turns.' There was a short silence and then they all laughed. After that they were less tense, less likely to have a row.

'Sorcha we don't know what's going on. We see you going out to these meetings and changing. We want to know what you do there. We're worried, that's all.' Her father made sure to speak this time, to break the turn system.

'It's not orgies, I can tell you,' said Sorcha, but good naturedly.

'Good. At least that's something,' said Eoin. 'But seriously, you seem to be very influenced by Roger. I don't think that he's that good an influence. He's a lot older. You're only fifteen, you know.'

'Do you think I'm going to get pregnant, or something?' asked Sorcha.

'You wouldn't be the first,' said Nuala. 'You have to be very careful, you know. No one ever intends to. But especially with older boys, they're more experienced and all. They can take advantage.'

'Roger and me aren't like that. It's all business, serious stuff.' As she said this Sorcha remembered kissing him earlier in the day.

'Hah. Famous last words. Everyone who's falling for someone says that. Especially if they shouldn't be falling for them,' said Eoin.

'Look, Sorcha, it's not natural that a girl your age ... ' Nuala decided to correct herself before Sorcha had time to do it for her, 'a teenager your age should be so serious about everything. You're supposed to be out having fun, experiencing life.'

'With a capital L, presumably. What is this life business? Am I supposed to be stupid and irresponsible because I'm fifteen? You just want me to carry on like all the others. To go a little wild, but safe harmless wild, or something. Then to settle down, like everyone else ... Like you.'

'Yes, that's the general idea, when you put it like that,' said Eoin. They were slipping back into turns again. They wanted to be fair to each other, to give each an equal chance.

'Well it's not what I want, to go to college, get a job. Hang on and watch the world decay, and so on. It's not what I want.'

'Has Roger been talking about college?' asked Nuala, worry in her voice.

'No, Roger never mentioned it. I just don't see the point at the moment, that's all.' She could see that this was not going down well so decided to say no more about it.

'What about Paul? Where does he fit in?' asked Eoin.

'Don't you approve of him either?'

'Of course we do. You know we like him. We wouldn't like you to be too serious about him, either, that's all. You're so young. You need to have lots of experience.' Nuala again.

'Of the right sort,' said Sorcha, heavy with irony.

'Actually, yes, of the right sort. We have learned something, you know, in life. We can try to protect you,' said Eoin.

'From what? The big bad wolf?'

'From yourself. From others who might take advantage of you.' Nuala spoke on cue.

'Fat chance Paul. He's a drip like that. He wouldn't want to do anything wrong, like sex or anything.'

'Actually, it's a relief to hear that. But what about Roger? He's strange.' Remembering about the turns, Nuala spoke again.

'You never met him,' said Sorcha.

'No, but from what you've said about him we've picked up things.'

'I'd better say nothing from now on,' said Sorcha, and decided to be as good as her word.

'That's not helpful. Anyway it's not just from what you've said. Pam has been talking about him as well.'

Sorcha said nothing.

'Look, for now, we're just advising you. But we'll want to know what's going on, Sorcha. We have to protect you, as I said,' said Eoin.

Sorcha was afraid that they would try to forbid her from going to meetings or seeing Roger so she changed her mind about keeping quiet. 'Look, I'll tell you what's happening, exactly. Then you'll see there's nothing to worry about. You'll have to trust me.'

'Hey, hold on,' said Eoin. 'We do trust you. Being concerned isn't the same as not trusting.'

'Sounds a lot like it,' said Sorcha. 'Look, I go to meetings of this group. There's people in it who are interested in saving the planet. Eoin - just like you, Dad - George, Brenda, Olivia, Roger and others. They come most often, I think. We discuss things, like how to recycle. Compost heaps and so on.'

'That sounds OK anyway,' put in Nuala, trying to keep the peace, and keep Sorcha going.

'Sometimes there's a particular issue, like maybe the Greenpeace ship is protesting and we send a letter of support. From the whole group.'

'Do you sign these?' asked cautious Eoin.

'Of course. I'd hardly sit there and be the only one not to sign. Anyway I'm not afraid to say what I believe.'

'It could come against you, if you ever wanted to get a visa to the US, say,' said Nuala, turn-taker.

'To hell with that,' said Sorcha, in her best John Wayne drawl. 'Anyway sometimes we do more, like the time we gave out the leaflets. That's it. There's nothing else. No drink, or smoking, or drugs. They don't approve of any of that. You'd be out of it if you did. They're strict, really. Like nuns.'

'What about sex?' asked Eoin, anxiously.

'I told you. Well maybe some of them do. I think maybe Brenda and one of the guys. She's very outspoken. She's in Trinity. She's really into animal rights and so on. That's her thing. She'd nearly have people who abuse animals strung up. She's very nice, though. She'd really make you think.'

'We're not keen on you being involved with people like that, Sorcha. They're older, aren't they?' Nuala asked.

'Yeh. I'm the youngest, I think.'

'You make it sound as if it's a religion for them,' said Eoin, 'and they're sleeping together. That's awful example for anyone your age.'

'Look, folks, it happens. I'm not. Paul and me don't. OK. Leave off, will you.' Sorcha was cross now, afraid that banning her from meetings was getting closer, and also a little afraid that they might be right. 'You have to trust me. Anyway,' her voice lowered here, 'it's my business what I do.'

'What's that you said, young lady?' Eoin said in his most astonished and threatening voice. Nuala was more direct in tone. She said, at the same time as Eoin, 'What did you say?'

'Nothing. It's my business what I do, that's all. It's my life.'
She was afraid that she had made a tactical mistake but they
seemed to take a more conciliatory approach.

'Sorcha, we're talking here about huge issues, not just washing dishes after dinner. We're talking about things that have
consequences and you being affected by these consequences.
We're your parents,' said Eoin.

'We have responsibility for you until you're grown up,' said
Nuala.

'I'll never be that, with you two,' said Sorcha.

'Look, there's no point in fighting. As I said a minute ago
we're only talking, for now. We just want you to think about
things, not get involved in anything stupid or dangerous. We're
not telling you what to do. But we will, if we have to,' said Eoin.

'That's not fair. You two sit there and you've decided everything before you even begin talking. What I say makes no
difference. You know it all.' Sorcha felt herself beginning to cry
and she didn't want to. She was upset because of them and they
would think it was because she was convinced by them and was
crying in regret for her wickedness. 'Zig and Zag,' she managed
to get out, as a shout. This surprised all three of them and again
they laughed. They did a bit of imitating for a few minutes and,
at least on the surface, they all felt better.

Then Nuala said, 'What happened the other night, with
Conor?'

Sorcha felt her stomach lurch. She was still confused about
that night. She certainly felt bad about it but Roger had told her
it was all right. That had helped, when she thought about what
he said. But still it worried her. She loved Conor and she had
been really enjoying talking to him and then suddenly, like a fire
bomb, she had been overcome and blown up. Everything had
been sucked into her, into the raging fire. She had completely
lost control. She wondered was this what would happen if she
was with Roger and the others. She couldn't fully accept what
Roger had told her, that everything was second to proper action
for the cause, as he and the others often called it. She knew that
she couldn't tell her parents about any of this. They wouldn't

understand: she was sure of that. How could they? It was so unusual, crazy even. She guessed that Conor would have told them a toned-down version of the row. Her father had seen her immediately afterwards, of course, but only for a few seconds. They wouldn't know how bad she had actually been.

'We had a row, that's all,' said Sorcha, with delicate understatement. She wasn't going to give anything away.

'We know that. We heard. Some of it anyway,' said Eoin. 'And besides, Conor was telling us. He was very upset. Whatever it was, he wouldn't tell us what you said to him.'

'I see,' said Sorcha quietly, not looking at her parents. She knew they might see how bad she felt about it if she did.

'Well, what happened?' asked Nuala, getting impatient.

'Look, I don't want to talk about it, it's between Conor and me, see,' said Sorcha, defiant again in the face of her mother's impatience with her.

'That's not good enough,' said Eoin, 'Conor is upset. We're supposed to be a family. He's worried about you. That's why he talked to us about it.'

'Look, Sorcha, this is what prompted us to have this talk with you in the first place,' said Nuala.

Sorcha said nothing. She didn't know what to say.

'You'll have to say something. Offer some explanation. It's simply not good enough that you behave this way,' said Eoin.

'What will I say then, if it's not good enough? What will I say?' Sorcha was getting angry.

'What we mean is you owe us an explanation of your behaviour with Conor. What did he do? Did he do anything to start the row or was it all your fault? Were you just being irrational?' said Nuala

'Oh, so I'm crazy now, is that it? That's what they used to do years ago. Lock up people that disagreed. Said they were crazy.'

'Don't be stupid, Sorcha,' said Eoin.

'Don't call me stupid,' said Sorcha.

'Sorcha, you're being ridiculous. You're certainly proving the point that we've a right to be worried about you. Now why did you attack Conor?' Nuala was almost getting out of her chair with impatience.

'I don't know why I did it. I don't know,' Sorcha shouted and sobbed. She jumped up and made to run out of the room but her father got to the door before her.

'Hold on,' he said gently. She stood in front of him for a moment and then said, 'Oh, Dad,' and leaned up against him. He held her to his chest and she let herself be enveloped in his warmth. 'It's OK. You're all right,' he said, the soothing sound of his voice so natural, so much part of her life since she had been a baby that she just wanted to sink under it and let it make everything fine again.

There was part of her, though, that knew that it was not that simple any more - that life could never be that simple again, where a father's arms and chest and voice could make all the confusion go away. She loved her father but knew that was not enough. After a while she slowly disengaged herself and said, 'I'll go to bed now, Dad, OK?' He said, 'Yes, love, do that,' and Sorcha thought she could hear sadness in his voice. She wondered if he too knew that he could no longer take care of her, that that was the past, her childhood.

17

Sorcha thought a lot about her conversation with her parents, over the next few days. She knew that her family was important to her. She didn't want to deny that. But she also knew that the feeling she'd had was right, that she was growing up and that she had to make her own life. She continued to find it all very difficult to come to terms with.

She wasn't really sure about Roger and the others. She believed that they were right in being concerned but she wondered, as she had lots of times, what they were really doing. She had heard a phrase recently. Hidden agenda. It was to do with the police and army in the North of Ireland operating in a way that contradicted their government's stated policy. It was underground, secret from the people, dangerous, hidden away but there all the same, influencing everything. It seemed to suit. When she was at meetings there often seemed to be a hidden agenda, one she didn't know about. Some of the others, the main group, Roger, Eoin, Brenda, George, Olivia and now and then a few others seemed always to have an understanding among them. It was as if they knew exactly how far to let discussions go. Often one of them would cut another off saying that they had gone far enough.

What troubled Sorcha was that Roger often seemed like that as well. Even when they were alone, he frequently seemed to be only half saying what was on his mind. His pauses and his long looks, which at the start had been like demands on her to be open and honest and mature, now sometimes seemed to her to be filled with shadowy ideas and schemes that were not for Sorcha's ears. Worse still, these silences appeared to be filled with silent judgements of her, of her concern about her family, her loyalty to Paul and Pam, as if these things were silly, childish, of the old way. Sorcha was not at all sure she supported the new way, where the planet, the group, the cause, were everything.

She saw Paul a few times. They got on well but didn't talk about their relationship. Sorcha felt a bit distant from him and he seemed to have the same feeling of strangeness towards her.

On Friday she was going to the shops for her mother when she met Roger.

'Where are you off to?' she asked.

'Oh, I was looking for you,' said Roger, smiling. With anyone else Sorcha would have taken that as a joke but with Roger she could not be sure.

'You can't live without me. I understand. But, Roger, I'm not free, can't you see that.' Sorcha was behaving the way she might with Paul, or anyone else and she usually did not joke in that way with Roger. Of course he took her seriously, or at least behaved as if he did.

'It's not that, Sorcha.' He was, as always looking at her, into her. It occurred to Sorcha that he hadn't denied what she had said. She wondered whether he was falling for her. Roger went on. 'I was just wondering how you were getting on, that's all.' So he hadn't been joking. He was looking for me, Sorcha thought.

'Actually, if you really want to know, I'm not getting on well at all. I'm fed up. No one seems to be able to accept me for what I am, to trust me.'

'Sorcha, I've told you, you must make your own decisions, stand alone. The family, capitalism, Western society don't allow people to be free. You must learn to be free.'

'Roger, what you say sounds great but ...' she hesitated.

Roger broke in, 'But what, Sorcha? There are no buts allowed. Everyone growing up has doubts about what they want. That's normal. If I thought that's all that was troubling you I wouldn't bother with you, but you're not just going through growing pains. You're different.'

'That's what my parents think, and they don't like it.'

'Of course they don't. Sorcha, you know that this world is rotten. Corruption is like a worm, or a fungus. It's rotting the structures of our society. It's even rotting the whole world, with their filthy pollution. Only some of us can see how bad it is. You can't expect ordinary people like your parents to understand.' Roger waited, still looking at her.

They were standing on Drumcondra Road, near the shops. The traffic, heavy as always thundered past. Every few moments a truck or bus with an out of condition engine engulfed their words with its whining impatience and left behind a pall of foul-smelling exhaust smoke. Roger didn't even need to comment, just to glance at the offending monsters. They were a forceful illustration of what he was telling her. The whole world suddenly seemed insane to Sorcha. Two people were trying to talk, a perfectly natural thing but they were standing on concrete surrounded by buildings, all of which had consumed huge amounts of the earth's resources when being built and had polluted its atmosphere, and all the time cars, trucks, buses, vans roared and puffed and ran and belched past, making their conversation nearly impossible, making the very act of breathing dangerous.

'Oh, what sort of a world is it?' Sorcha nearly sobbed out to Roger.

He waited a moment to allow a truck time to pass, and said, 'It's the only one we've got. And it's up to us to save it.' He waved his hand, taking in the drivers and everyone else. 'They won't do it. Look.' A car was passing and the driver, in a white shirt and a tie, his jacket neatly hanging at the back window, was talking urgently into his car-phone. His eyes were darting around, looking for the space into which he thrust his car, to gain two or three metres. 'He's not interested. Him or his type. They're even prepared to be killed or kill to get somewhere in a hurry. They talk on their phones so as not to waste precious time. They're stupid. Don't they see that the only thing they're wasting is the planet. Their lives. All of our lives, Sorcha. Yours and mine as well. And nobody cares. Except us.'

Sorcha was swept into agreement with Roger. Everyone else seemed to admire the hard work of all these people. They got up early, went to bed late, talked, made deals. Most of them were making products that were dangerous and harmful.

'Do you know, I read somewhere that in some cities the average speed of cars is now only eight miles an hour, because of the traffic,' Sorcha said.

'It would be funny, if it wasn't so stupid,' said Roger.

'Roger, I don't want to go on like this. I don't want my life to be the same, just fitting in to the old pattern. But what can I do? I'm going back to school in a few weeks, then it's more study, university. Then I'm in. I get a job and I'm like everyone else.'

'No, you're not. You're not like everyone else. I told you, if you were I wouldn't bother with you. And it doesn't have to be like that.'

Sorcha felt almost grateful to Roger. He looked so plain, so uninteresting, nothing special about his slightly odd looks but he was so strong. He knew about life. And he cared for her. She was not sure whether she wanted to grab him and kiss him or cry on his shoulder, let him put his arms around her and mind her, or sit down somewhere and talk to him forever.

'There are some people, Sorcha, who think like us.' Sorcha noticed the word 'us'. She felt, again, included by what Roger was saying. 'Some of us have decided that we are not going to be part of all the corruption and destruction. You know us, Sorcha. You've met us at the meetings. We have other meetings, as well.' He stopped.

Sorcha was afraid to breathe. The traffic and its noise seemed to have faded away. She could hear her own heart pounding with excitement. She had known there was something. Now Roger was going to tell her, include her in this secret knowledge.

'No one knows about this, Sorcha, except the people who are members. We're a group of committed people. We have the other meetings, the ones you come to, to get as many people involved in as many issues as possible. But we're separate. We meet separately, have a separate agenda.' The words hidden agenda flashed into Sorcha's mind, making her momentarily uneasy. 'We are committed to making this world a better place for everyone. We know that this will involve a change in society and that everyone will not want it. There will have to be sacrifices. When you called the other night I spoke to you about that. We were meeting then, in my house. That's why I couldn't delay with you. We discussed you afterwards and agreed to tell you about us.'

'Go on.'

'Sorcha, it's not just talk. We're committed to changing the world. That means doing things, action. People will have to learn that they must sacrifice some of their luxurious ways. We,' he stressed the 'we', 'will have to teach them.'

A huge truck with double trailer charged by, going far too fast, had to brake hard, hissing and snorting, and just managed to keep in control, leaving a trail of rubber on the road.

'Go on,' said Sorcha.

'I've said enough. Too much for now. Now you know. Are you shocked, Sorcha?'

'No. I don't think so. Not at all. It's exciting.'

18

It was Molly who put forward the idea, which everyone agreed was unusual for her, as the general consensus was that she had not a brain in her head. She suggested that the gang organise a Great End of Summer Holiday Party. The idea was delightedly pounced on and within minutes plans were being made.

Sorcha first heard of it when Paul called to her house. She hadn't been with the gang when the idea was brought up. Sorcha had been spending less and less time with the rest of them. She found that they just didn't fit in with her interests any more.

'What do you think? It'll be a laugh,' said Paul, full of enthusiasm.

'Suppose so,' said Sorcha, not feeling much enthusiasm at all. 'Who'll be there?'

'Oh, everyone. Whoever we want. Bop, bop a loo bop bop.' He danced appropriately before sliding his arm around her waist. 'And slow and smoochy as well,' he said, nuzzling up to her.

'Go away, you creep.' Sorcha pushed him away but was laughing, despite herself.

'It'll be gas. Give us something to look forward to before we go back into the valley of death, having to fight off on all sides the tyrants of Biology, Geography, History, Tyranny, Muckology, Rubbishology and many, many other ologies, not to mention the hordes of teachers armed with mighty sticks of chalk of many glorious colours and boards of matted black, and projectors, overhead, underhead and videos of plays and videos of the dissected inner organs of bulls and frogs and of bullfrogs and videos of volcanoes, and rain forests, and videos of tundras and outer space and inner space ... '

Sorcha was laughing at Paul, getting into his mood, 'And we will gain strength from our opulent and meticulously planned and lavish and triumphant Great End of Summer Holiday Party...'

Paul interrupted '... to which we will have invited experts from every field, outstanding in the art of copying of homework, outstanding in the myriad skills of presenting projects containing no information, outstanding spoofs, charlatans, outstanding and respected licks, swots, distracters of teachers, inventors of the most plausible of excuses in highly difficult situations ... '

'Those outstanding in the corridor for being constantly caught. And we will use the expertise of these great experts to fight off the onslaught of the trials and tribulations of the all-powerful School Year until ... ' Sorcha was now standing on a chair, her voice dramatically loud, as if she was a great orator from ancient times delivering a wonderfully heroic speech. She clutched imaginary garments to her and held an imaginary staff of authority outstretched in her right hand.

Paul was on one knee in front of her, now her faithful subject. He said, '... until we are finally engulfed by the all-powerful Leaving Certificate Examination.' With that he stopped.

Sorcha leaped from the chair and knelt beside Paul and cradled his head to her, as if minding him. 'Poor, poor Paul. How awful.' She quickly changed her tone. 'Hah! I don't have to do that stinking thing for two lovely years.'

'One and three quarters, actually, you rat.' Paul pushed her down on the floor and tried to pin her shoulders. She rolled aside and jumped up. 'Not so easy, varlet,' she said and as he tried to stand she pulled his leg, sending him sprawling. She grabbed a cushion from an easy chair, plonked it on his back and sat down hard.

'Aargh, release me, you heathen savage, or I'll call the wrath of the gods on you,' Paul shouted.

'Never!' cried Sorcha, 'Never, as long as I have blood in my veins.'

Paul was pushing hard against her and Sorcha was turning over just as the door opened. Her mother was there. She stood in some surprise, not really able to think of what to say. Sorcha sat on the floor and Paul sat up slowly, trying, not very successfully, to look dignified. After a few moments Nuala said, half apologetically, half accusingly, 'I was just wondering what the noise was.' She went out, saying, rather primly, 'I thought wrestling matches were long finished in this house.'

When the door shut Paul and Sorcha looked at each other and then laughed. They were shaken by the laughter. From deep inside it filled them until they were helpless, shaking, falling on the floor, on each other, unable to get up, or to stop, until their breath was gone, their stomachs ached, their eyes watered. As the storm subsided gradually, they knelt on the floor in a silence that was punctuated by giggles from one or the other. Sorcha wiped the tears from her eyes and looked at Paul. She was about to speak, but he stomped over to her on his knees and put his arms around her. All the tension between them seemed to have vanished as if by magic. She kissed him, full of excitement and love for him. She felt his lips pressing on hers, felt his tongue, moist and beautiful.

They were still aware of her mother about, possibly even listening in the hall, so strange their behaviour must have appeared to her. 'Let's go for a walk,' Sorcha said. They fixed their tossed clothes and walked out, arms around each other comfortably for the first time in what seemed like ages.

They called to Simone and Jeff's house. 'Hey, look who's here. It's Ms Environmentally Friendly of the 1990s. We are honoured,' said Jeff when he opened the door. Sorcha did not reply, just smiled and said, 'Hi, Jeff.' Paul said, 'Shut up,' and Sorcha could see him warning Jeff with a look. Paul didn't want Jeff's slagging to ruin Sorcha's new mood. Sorcha reckoned that the chances of Jeff being sensitive to a look from anyone, unless it was a come-on from a girl, were pretty slim. Simone came out to the hall.

'Oh, Hi, Paul. Hi, Sorcha. Long time no see.'

'Hi, Sim,' said Sorcha.

'Hiya, babe,' said Paul in a sultry movie-style voice.

Simone and Jeff had already been discussing the party.

'The first thing to sort out,' said Jeff, 'is where to have the blasted thing. It's a pity Miley's Place is gone. We could have used that.'

'Yeh, some chance. When it came down to it you'd have been afraid,' said Paul.

'Anyway that creep Roger lives there with his organic potatoes now. The smell must be yucky,' said Simone.

Paul was not keen to let the subject of Roger interfere at this stage but before he could say anything Jeff said, 'That guy is weird. I saw him and some others the other day unloading stuff from a car and I said, "Hi, Rog," all friendly like, and he just looked through me, as if he'd never seen me before. One of the others said, "Who's the kid?" or some crap like that and he just said, "Oh, no one," and went back to taking the stuff from the car. Cartons of some sort, and paint, it was.'

'Creep,' said Simone.

Paul wanted to get back to discussing the party so he said, knowingly, 'Look, Jeff, it's obvious whose house we'll use.'

'Whose?' asked Jeff, puzzled for a moment.

'It's obvious,' said Paul, more pointedly.

'Oh yes, I get it,' said Jeff. 'Molly is the one. She came up with the idea, she comes up with the house. Clever boy, Paul. Now, how'll we persuade little miss Molly? Any idea?'

'Tell her she's a genius, she'll do anything for you,' suggested Simone.

'Nasty, nasty,' said Sorcha.

'Sorry, anything except that,' Simone said, fluttering her eyelids. They all laughed.

'Molly it is,' said Jeff, 'Let's go around now and get her to make the suggestion. Leave it to old Jeff, he knows how to handle her.'

It didn't prove too difficult and Molly was able to get agreement from her parents. The others always claimed that they spoilt her because they hadn't been able to give her any brains. They were well off and lived in a big house. Molly's parents agreed to provide the place, subsidise the cost of the food and, best of all, go to the theatre for the evening.

They decided on the next Saturday, the last weekend before school started. Everyone in the gang had to contribute money and they invited others from their schools, who wouldn't have to pay. They spent a few days making lists, pricing, buying supplies and getting the place ready. They were inviting, as well as the nine members of the gang, eleven others. They decided that twenty was an acceptable number. Any more and Molly's parents would have been likely to object.

'There'll probably be crashers anyway,' said Pam.

'What's that?' Sonny wanted to know.

'People who come, who aren't invited,' said Jeff, 'Big nasties, causing trouble. They'll most likely break up the place, smash the furniture and so on. It's one of the risks you take, throwing a party, the downside, Sonny. Still.' he was looking at Molly to see how she was reacting. She seemed a little pale to Jeff.

'Don't mind him, Molly,' said Paul, putting her arm around her. 'I'll take care of everything. My little brother got a new baseball bat and I'll bring it.' He mimed swinging a bat. 'Swipe, swipe. Take that.'

'This is the guy who was afraid of a gick-head ticket seller in town, now let's not forget that,' said Jeff.

'Now, hold on. Paul was very brave that day. And he's got so strong since then,' simpered Simone.

'Now, hold on,' said Molly, 'gate crashers are serious. My parents won't let us have the party if there are gate crashers.'

'Molly, Molly, Molly,' Jeff said, false patience filling his voice, 'if we knew in advance they were coming, they wouldn't be crashers, would they?'

'I suppose not.' Molly sounded unsure.

'Makes perfect sense,' said Paul crisply.

'Seems to,' said Sorcha. 'Don't worry Molly. There'll be no trouble.' Then she could not resist a joke. 'If it makes you feel better, we won't invite any crashers.'

The others all agreed loudly and Molly was a little more satisfied.

'What about the booze, the beer, you know. Ooh, la, la. Let's have some fun.' Jeff was singing.

'No way. Definitely out. I'd be killed,' said Molly. Jeff looked hurt.

'No, she's right,' said Paul. 'We don't need it anyway, stupid stuff.'

'Have you tried it?' asked Simone. 'It makes you feel good, really good.'

'Well, I've had a little at home, you know, a glass or two, that's all.'

'I bet you've never really had a drink at all Paul, not a real one.'

'I told you. I don't want any more. It's stupid. It's a drug.' Paul was defensive. He knew lots of people his age drank and he didn't really want to, but he didn't want to seem stupid or babyish either.

Sorcha said, 'Look, Sim, if you want to, or Jeff, that's your business. But people have to stand up for themselves, make their own lives. Leave Paul alone. Alcohol is a dangerous drug. Let him be himself.'

'Yeh, that's right,' said Paul. He looked at her, grateful that she had got him off the hook for now, and that she cared enough about him to do it.

The party went ahead on Saturday, as planned. Pam and Sorcha had come over early to help Molly get organised and they were there for a while before any of the others arrived. Sorcha, for a few days, had got caught up in organising the party and in all the fun and joking. By now she was getting a bit tired of it all. All of Jeff's jokes were the same. Everyone wanted to laugh and push and shout all the time. No one seemed to want to think about anything. If she heard anyone say they wanted to have a good time again she felt she'd throttle them. She thought that a good time was a way of describing something after it had happened. You'd either had a good time or not, while you were doing something else, like going walking or going to the pictures.

She couldn't see how you planned an activity called a good time. It seemed so stupid to her that she could hardly express it. She'd been having a good time but by the time she got to the day of the party she wasn't so sure that she still was.

She had met Roger only once during the preparations and would have liked to talk to him about it but had been afraid that he would disapprove, or even sneer at her about it, so she had said nothing.

When people started to arrive they hung around talking in groups. Everyone was a little uncomfortable. They all knew that it would take a while to relax. Jeff came and he immediately began making jokes and slagging. Soon others joined in and the atmosphere warmed up. 'Let's dance,' shouted Jeff and grabbed Molly.

Sorcha was standing beside Paul, holding his hand. 'He's been drinking.'

'Simone too. I couldn't get close enough to smell it. She'd probably jump all over me if I tried.' Simone was wearing a really short tight skirt and lots of make up. 'Listen to her voice though. I think it's slurred. Jeff's too. Look at him.' The music was fast and Jeff was leaping like a half-crazy puppy. 'I just hope they don't cause any hassle.'

'Ah, they won't,' said Sorcha.

They danced for a while and then moved separately about the room. Sorcha chatted to some of the crowd from school. They asked her how she was getting on. She was relieved to have a change of people to talk to and told them what she had been doing over the summer. They seemed to be listening and, delighted with an interested audience, which she rarely had these days, she explained the reasons why she was concerned about the planet and its problems. She had to shout somewhat over the music and general noise.

'Look, Sorcha's off again,' Paul said to Pam.

'What do you mean?' Pam asked.

'She's got those poor folks in the corner, lecturing them, no doubt.'

'Maybe you're being unfair. They could be talking about you, how handsome you are,' Pam teased.

'Probably. But no, look, she's really serious, at a party and all.' Sorcha did look as if she was really serious, her face alive with feeling, her arms slicing the air.

They talked on and then danced, then talked some more.

Sorcha had stopped talking to the small group, as they had drifted off to dance or to other people. She had been watching Pam and Paul for a while. They seemed to be getting on very well. When they were dancing they would lean over to each other and speak and then laugh easily. When they were not dancing they laughed all the time.

As a song came to an end Jeff announced, loudly, 'The first smoochy one of the night. Grab your partners, but be decent.' Sorcha expected Paul to come over and was half-rising off the floor where she had been sitting. She was taken aback when he and Pam, who had been dancing, slid their arms around each other and swayed gently to the music. She felt a lurch inside, knew it again as jealousy. Why did it have to come, when you were fed up anyway, to make it all worse? she thought. Of course that is when jealousy tends to strike, when people are lacking confidence, when they feel insecure.

She waited until near the end of the party and then got a chance to take Paul aside. 'You're a swine,' she began.

She sounded serious to Paul, so he decided to say nothing for the moment. It was easier, because he felt that she was probably right and to say anything would make it worse. He was not feeling good.

'We're supposed to be going with each other and you spend the whole night with my best friend. You're rotten, you really are.'

'Now hold on, Sorcha. I only started talking to Pam because you were having a debate with Mary and the others.'

'What do you mean, "a debate"? We were chatting for a few minutes, that's all and that's ages ago anyway. You ran off on me.'

'No, I didn't. I was here. I was only talking to Pam for a while.'

'Ages. And it was lots more than talk over there.' Sorcha indicated the dancing area. 'You're just getting fed up with me. You want novelty, that's all. You're such a typical ... boy.'

'Bloody hell. That's not fair. None of it is.'

'Yes it is.'

'No it's not. You're off with that crowd all the time and then you seem to be all right again, for the party, in the last few days and then tonight you're in a mood again and then yap-yap-yap with them in the corner. What am I to do?'

'If that's the way you feel then really this is all silly. You either accept me as I am or we'll end it, Paul.'

'No. Wait a bit.' Paul was worried by that. 'It's not that. You're changing, Sorcha. I've told you that. Pam agrees.' He was sorry he had said that. 'Everyone does.' He was sorry he had said that too. It made it sound as if he was discussing her with everyone, which he wasn't, really.

'So, I've changed. You're supposed to change at our age. It's called growing up. Some people want to stay babies for ever.' She looked around the room, and then back at Paul.

'Yeh, well, there's growing up and being stupid. You don't want to have fun, to have a good time. I do.'

Sorcha sighed. Here it was again, the good time. 'Well, have a good time then, without me.'

'No. Why not with you? You've been fun again. Yourself. Now you've changed back. It's the real you I like.'

'Paul, I don't even know what's the real me, any more. That's the truth.' She felt herself getting sad, no longer angry or jealous. 'Why can't you see that?'

'It's OK, Sorcha. It's OK.' She leaned against him. They kissed and danced to a slow song. Sorcha was not sure about anything, as she had said to Paul, but this felt better than being jealous did, so it would do at least for the time being.

Pam was dancing with one of the boys from Paul's school. He was annoying her, holding her tight and pulling her towards him. His face was on her neck and she could feel his breath, hot and damp. She wasn't even sure if his name was John or Joe and she had no interest in being this close to him. She supposed that he thought he was being irresistible. Why, she wondered, could boys not try using their brains and just talk to a girl, instead of grabbing at them at every opportunity. To make it worse she could see, over his shoulder, Paul dancing with Sorcha.

She had watched them talking and at first she thought they were having a row. Sorcha's face had looked as if it was backed by a thunder storm. Paul looked unsure, scared of her, she thought. Then suddenly Sorcha's face had changed, had collapsed into misery and she had slumped against Paul. Since then they had danced and kissed, as if they were the only ones in the whole world, never mind the whole room.

Pam was jealous. She admitted that to herself. She had fallen for Paul in a big way and from listening to him talking she had really thought that he was fed up with Sorcha. Now she wondered was he just going on with all that stuff to make her feel sorry for him and to fall for him. How could she trust boys? She never knew what was really going on. She had often talked to Sorcha about it, although not so much recently, and they agreed that most of them were really only interested in a thrill. Not that Pam objected to a thrill herself, but it had to be with someone special, not just like it was for this John, or Joe. For him, Pam could be anyone at all. She felt a shudder of revulsion going through her. John, or Joe must have interpreted it differently because he moaned and started to move his hands. Luckily the track ended just then and Pam said, 'Thanks. Bye.' She quickly disentangled herself and walked to the other side of the room. John, or Joe, stood there like half an apple, incomplete and on the verge of toppling over. Unable to understand why the girl had left so suddenly. He had been doing so well.

19

Sorcha had been back in school for four days. The party was a week behind her. Paul's parents were insisting, right from the start, that he could only go out at weekends, and not even on Sunday nights, for the whole year. Paul agreed with them. He told Sorcha that if he was going to get the points in the Leaving Cert that he needed to qualify for medicine in College then he would have to get started straight away. That meant work every night, during the day at weekends and early nights in bed all the time. 'Miserable, I know, but it'll be worth it in the end. Yes, doctor, no doctor, shall I suture the opening, Doctor? I hope so anyway.' Paul had said, 'making the most of it' as he put it. No one expected quite as much from Sorcha, as she was in fifth year, traditionally one of partial rest. Her mother and father had warned her not to get too relaxed and fall behind. They were looking for plenty of study and they let her know. Sorcha knew they were right if she wanted to get points for university but as she was increasingly sure that she did not want to go there she had a correspondingly decreasing interest in the points.

She had seen Paul only once since the party, on Sunday. He had been very caring and had asked her how she was. He wanted to know did she still love him. She told him that she would hardly have stopped since the night before.

'That's true, I suppose,' he said.

'That doesn't mean, Paul that everything is solved. I'm not going to be someone just for you. I have to be myself. You'll have to love me for it.'

'I know,' he said, quite miserably.

Now it was Saturday, and she had decided to go for a walk. She had got the bus to Rathfarnham and was making her way up Three Rock, for the first time in ages. She had stopped going there during the summer, once she had decided not to use buses any more. Now she decided to make an exception because she really wanted this walk.

She loved the way the path wound its way up the mountain and the occasional glimpses through the trees of the television masts, the sea far below, or the countryside, the farms and further away, the suburban houses.

Earlier, when still on the road, she had passed the gates of a big house. There were two huge pillars and one massive black iron gate. The driveway curved to the house, almost out of sight behind the twin rows of young poplar trees. On one of the pillars was a push button intercom system and on the other was mounted a conspicuous security camera. Sorcha had never paid too much attention to the house before but now, on the mountain, she thought about it and tried to imagine the people who lived there. Rich surely. They must be rich. They wanted people to know. And scared. Why else all the security? What were they scared of? Robbery? Kidnap? If they didn't show off people would not know about them and they wouldn't be targets. She decided they were typical of society. They had gathered huge wealth, probably at the expense of the environment and their badly paid workers, and now were living in a fortress, afraid of the world they exploited. They were right to be. Some day it would strike back. Some day the planet would give up on them, refuse them food and air, choke them. The only trouble with that, she thought, was that the rest of us would suffer as well.

Roger was right. These people needed to be taught a lesson before we were all destroyed. They would deserve it, if they were kidnapped. She wouldn't feel one bit sorry for them, that's for sure.

Sorcha reached the top and wedged herself between two rocks, under the presence of the television masts behind her, still thinking about the people in the house and about others like them. She thought about all of the people in all the houses of the city spread out way below her. Not for the first time she thought of the sea nibbling at the edge of the city, of how it was slowly dying because of the sludge and sewage and junk that was being dumped in it. She thought of the radioactivity in it, caused by the nuclear reprocessing plant across the Irish Sea. She wondered about the fishermen, and their families, out there in their boats, sailing back into Howth, as she had often seen them. Were they bringing back food or deadly toxins? Were the people who ate their fish being destroyed because of the stupidity of others. Those men had to work, had to earn a living. There was a girl in school whose father was a fisherman in Howth, who could be out there even as she looked. The girl was ordinary, normal, meant no harm, was no monster.

Roger was right. People will not change, she thought. They will have to be encouraged, be taught. 'Wow,' said Sorcha out loud, 'Paul would flip, really flip if he heard me thinking like this.' She thought of all the crowd at the party. They'd all flip. They'd think she was crazy. She knew, though, that if she was serious then she could not think like that. She didn't care, really, if that was what they thought. Things would have to be done.

Roger was right. He had said that his group were 'committed people.' That was what was needed. She would be committed. There was no other way. She let her eye follow the line from south of Bray along the coast to Howth and hazily northwards towards Drogheda. Then she stood up and walked around to where she could look down at the rest of the city, the northern suburbs, the west, the south city. Hundreds and hundreds of thousands of people, the same sun, warm and life-giving, shining on them all. Yes, she would be committed to protecting them, to saving them. She turned to head back down the mountain, back to the city.

Some people get an idea into their heads and it is fixed there, like a huge monument. They come to worship their idea and think that everyone who disagrees with it is bad or evil. Soon they see nothing but their wonderful pillar rising up blocking out the sky. Others always question things. They are attracted to the solidity and certainty of a great fixed idea, one that shows clearly what is right and wrong for all time. But still they question, and their questioning eventually shows other angles, other ways of looking at the world. The monument is chopped away at its foundation, and eventually is nothing more than a ruin, a memory of what was. Sorcha was standing under her monument, hiding in its shade, but she was a questioner at heart, deep down. The knowledge that her friends and family would, quite seriously, think that she was mad never fully left her.

While she was walking down towards home the transmitter behind her was sending out its signals. Stories were gathered from around the world and were beamed out as news to nearly every house in the city. When she got in, the evening bulletin was on and she flopped into an easy chair, tired from her long walk. 'Hi, Dad. Anything happening?'

'Something about Greenpeace in the headlines. I didn't quite catch it. In the Pacific. A nuclear protest, I think, and some sort of trouble.' Sorcha waited but there was no more about it. She flicked the channels, looking for information. She was as concerned as if it was news about someone she knew, a relative. Finally she heard it. The Greenpeace ship that travelled the world highlighting environmental problems had been protesting at a nuclear test site in the Pacific. A warhead was due to be exploded and the ship had sailed right into the centre of the site. They had done this before but this time the French navy had sailed in after them, taken over the ship, arrested the crew and the bomb had been set off.

Sorcha jumped up, as soon as the report was over, and rushed out. She called, 'I'll be back later.'

'What about dinner?' shouted her father.

'I'll get it later,' as the door closed.

Nuala came into the room and Eoin told her that Sorcha was gone. Nuala wanted to know where.

'I don't know. She muttered and gasped her way through the news and then jumped up and shot out the door.'

'Roger, I suppose,' said Nuala.

Sorcha knocked at Roger's door. She rarely called, usually meeting him outside, and was still nervous doing it. His mother answered. She was a strange woman, tall and so skinny she was hardly there. Her hair was long and straight, she wore a crinkly blouse, the waistcoat of a man's suit and an ankle-length loose skirt. Her feet were bare. Her hands glanced out from under rings of gold and silver, two or even three to a finger. She said nothing to Sorcha when she asked, hesitatingly, if Roger was there. Roger's mother turned away and called out, 'Hey, one of your kid friends is here,' as she walked into the kitchen at the end of the hall.

Sorcha wasn't sure whether to go in through the wide open door or to stay on the doorstep. She did not have to be indecisive for long as Roger came down the stairs, towelling his hair dry. He looked in good humour, which was a relief to Sorcha, as she could never be sure of Roger's humours in advance.

'Did you hear?' Sorcha burst out. 'It's been on, just now.' She could hardly contain herself. Sorcha was feeling, for the first time in her life, real anger about something completely outside of herself. Her life was, obviously, not affected by what had happened but the injustice of it so filled her up that she could hardly speak. She felt like striking out, like hitting someone really hard. If she could have got her hands on the French navy at that point she would quite probably have attacked some member of it.

She blurted the story out to Roger who had heard nothing of it.

'Hey, calm down,' he said and invited her in. 'Look,' said Roger, 'these things happen all the time. Governments don't want the boat rocked. They won't allow serious protest. If you're going to be involved you have to get used to the idea. People get into trouble for doing nothing wrong. It's a pain, but it's what you learn to expect. Just take it easy, OK?'

'Yeh, I suppose so. But I'm so mad. Really I am. Why can't they protest? That's legal. They have a right.'

'Not in law, not to do that. It's government property and they were trespassing on it.'

'It's the world's property. People don't care about the nuclear issue any more. They think it's all over since the Americans and Russians made up. But look. Remember the Gulf War. They were talking about using the things against Iraq at one point,' argued Sorcha.

'I know. Of course you're right. It's just that you have to learn to keep a grip, put things in perspective. We must be in control. That's all I'm saying. Don't blow this up to be more than it is.' Roger smiled at his unintentional pun. 'Excuse the joke.'

Sorcha smiled, glad to hear Roger making a rare joke, even if it was by accident.

'The time has come, Sorcha,' said Roger, in a voice so serious that all trace of his humour vanished instantly, 'for you to decide. We do take things seriously.' As before, he stressed the 'we'. 'Do you want to join us? Do you want to join the Circle?' For the first time, he named his group. Sorcha was silenced. No more hints. They, he, wanted her in. Right in. No messing. This was the inner group. Not just handing out leaflets but changing things. The way to a better future. A world to be proud of, not scared of. Air to breathe, not to choke on. She would be part of this change. No sitting on the fence, like Paul and Pam, like her parents, complaining of pollution, doing nothing. They would make people sit up and take notice.

'Yes, Roger, I'm in.' Her face was ablaze. She was beautiful.

Roger, who usually did not respond to the things on the surface, such as appearance, felt that this beauty was from inside Sorcha and hugged her to him. 'Sorcha, we're having a get-together, a sort of party. On next Saturday night. You'll come. You can really meet the others.'

Sorcha laughed, to herself. She had been unwilling to tell Roger about the gang's party, in case he laughed and now he was inviting her to a party of his own. This, though, would be different. Older people. Thoughtful people. Real people. No dancing and grabbing. This would be sophisticated. Still, she decided not to say anything about the Great End of Holiday Party. He might not see the humour of the contrast as she saw it.

For Sorcha all doubt had gone. She had been accepted, purely on her own merits. No one was going to sneer at her, think she was mad. It was special. Roger had insisted that she actually swear not to tell anybody at all about his group. She still had to be formally admitted, but that would be at the next meeting. She had felt strange swearing, saying the words after him, but once she had done it she knew how serious it all was, how she would never let down the Circle. Never.

20

'They're out. I swear. Moggy said it.' Dearbhla was in a state of consternation and excitement. She came bursting into Sorcha's classroom between Irish and French class, uniform tie pulled down, top button of her blouse open and her hair, clipped up in the morning, now half undone and trailing at one side. Dearbhla could never be tidy but was one of those people who looked great when she was in a mess so no-one ever minded. If anyone else wore their uniform the way she did they'd get detention points.

She was talking about the Inter Cert results and the effect was similar to that of an announcement that there was a bomb in the room. Every single person in the class jumped out of their seats and all began shouting at once ... When? Where? Are you sure? Who said it? Are they good? Oh no, I'll be killed! ... Noise filled the room almost to bursting point. Teachers arrived and succeeded in subduing them. An uneasy wait followed while the results were checked and then, after an hour or so, they were released to the principal's office where they queued in agony for their envelopes. Sorcha watched each student coming out. Some opened the envelope, ripping the paper, hands shaking. The results could be seen in their reactions. Some leaped in the air, some smiled and some, depressingly, were grim faced and silent, or smiled bravely but weakly. Others put the unopened envelopes away and walked out to privacy, trying to look unconcerned, or were embarrassed by the whole procedure.

Sorcha was with Pam. 'I'm not opening mine within earshot of here.'

'Me neither.'

Finally, envelope in her schoolbag, Sorcha went to the park. There were other students there, like herself, who had come to be on their own. She sat by the river, her feet dangling. I can always jump in, if they're awful, she thought, grinning into the knee-deep, sluggish water.

* * *

She came into the house at teatime. Her parents were there.

'Well?' asked Nuala.

Sorcha smiled. 'As in Science, History, Geography, Maths. Bs in English, French, Spanish, Commerce. C in Irish.'

They were delighted. The three of them talked each other down for ages before Eoin finally asked Sorcha why she hadn't phoned them. She had no answer. It simply had not occurred to her. She had opened the envelope and had been pleased and then had gone for a long walk and never even thought of phoning anyone. Nuala and Eoin were so happy with the results that they said nothing, although Sorcha could see that they were hurt.

'Oh, no. Pam! I never phoned her either. How did she do?'

'You don't know how Pam did? Sorcha, that's terrible. What sort of friend are you?' accused Nuala, her tone genuinely incredulous.

'Paul. Did you ring him?' asked Eoin anxiously. He could see by her expression that she had not. 'You'd better use the phone, genius. See you later,' he said, not terribly kindly. They left her on her own.

Pam was, naturally, upset. 'Where were you? I thought something had happened. First I thought you'd failed, then I thought you were dead.'

Once again, Sorcha could not explain herself. 'Sorry, Pam. I've no excuse.'

'I thought you were my friend.'

Sorcha did not answer. Finally they agreed, not very warmly, to meet later. The class was going into town to celebrate. They decided to go along to see what would happen. Some of the others had given out to them for not going in June when the Inter was over. Anyway, Pam was more enthusiastic about celebrating this time, having her own good results as fuel.

After that phone call she could not face ringing Paul and decided to call around to him. She knew that he'd be annoyed and she supposed that he had a right to be. Yet in a way she didn't care. Really, the results were not that important to her, so it was not as if she was keeping something vital from him. She had felt very little until she got home and met her parents and even then it was as much the infection of their excitement as the results themselves which affected her. Yet everyone did think it was important and she couldn't really pretend that it meant nothing at all to her. Paul would accuse her of not caring about anyone. She knew she would feel bad about that and that it wasn't true. Was she not joining the Circle precisely because she cared about people, deeply?

She was right. Paul was upset.

'Pam was around. She did well.' Emphasis on 'she'. 'She was worried about you. At least she cares about you, even if you don't care about her any more.'

There was no point in arguing. Seen from his point of view he was completely right. The only explanation for her behaviour that made sense was that she didn't care about anyone except herself. And yet, that was not at all how she had felt. She had wanted time on her own, time to savour the experience of the results. She was moving on to something new. This was not to be repeated. It was the one and only time that she would do the Inter. It was the last Inter ever so no one else would ever again be in her exact position. She was sorry that she had not phoned everyone, and said so to Paul, but she didn't bother him with her need to be on her own. She did not want even to try to explain it. Not for the first time, she was unsure how to deal with confusing and contradictory feelings, which seemed to have complete freedom to do as they liked inside her.

Paul accepted her apology. 'Well, you've done it. The Last Intier. Get it? Last Frontier, Last Intier.' He laughed at his deliberately corny joke.

'Will you come with us?'

'Can't. Have to study. The Leavingtier and all that.'

Sorcha wondered if he was complaining because he didn't seem to be important enough to her, how it was that he would not give up one night of study to be with her, especially when he'd had the afternoon off school because of the results, and had done a few extra hours then.

'Is Paul not with you?' were Pam's first words when they met later on. Sorcha wondered why she was asking. After all Pam had called around to him earlier. She could be after Paul, Sorcha remembered. She told her that he wasn't coming and apologised again for not contacting her earlier about the results.

'Forget about it, Sorcha. Let's have a good time,' said Pam.

The girls from school were meeting some boys from the local boys' school in a pub in town. Sorcha and Pam knew it was a place that would serve under age people. Some of their classmates would drink, maybe even get drunk.

'Let's get paralytic,' said Pam.

'Yeh, letch. We'll have a fhew littul dhrindsh i' ordher to schelevrate.' Sorcha was walking very carefully, as if she was drunk and trying not to fall down. They had just come to the bus stop on Drumcondra Road, at the place where Roger had first hinted at the Circle. A woman already waiting glanced in their direction.

Sorcha whispered, quite loudly, to Pam, 'She schthinksh we're sherioush-ly dhrunkhe, sho she doesh. Pam.'

Pam said, aloud, 'Sho she doesh, Sshorcha-sh, sho she doesh.' She leaned against the bus stop with her shoulder and slid off, stumbling and almost falling to the ground. The bus arrived and they stood back elaborately to let the woman board ahead of them. 'Afhther you, madam,' said Sorcha, bowing. 'Yesh, afther you-sh, madahm,' said Pam.

The woman spoke, shocked, to the driver as she paid her fare, 'It's terrible. I'm sure they've just got their Inter results. All dressed up and drunk as tarts. Disgusting. I blame their parents.'

Pam and Sorcha, partly afraid that they wouldn't be let on the bus and partly to confuse the woman and the driver, who looked as if he agreed fully with her, jumped nimbly up the steps, asking for their tickets in bright, cheery and very sober voices. The driver was puzzled and looked after the woman who was taking her seat. As they passed Sorcha said brightly, 'Lovely evening,' to the woman who scowled horribly at her.

There was a big crowd in the pub. They were excited and had begun singing. A good few had pints of beer, and one or two of the boys were already showing signs of being drunk. They were not as bad as Sorcha and Pam had pretended to be but were getting there.

Sorcha said to Pam, 'Look, they think it's great to drink. In an hour they'll be throwing up all over someone and tomorrow they'll boast about it. And you know, they'll all pretend to believe each other.'

'Yeh. Still Sorcha, it might be fun.'

'What, to have someone puke on your new tights?'

'No, stupid. To have a drink, to try it.'

'Be my guest. Don't expect me to carry you home to your parents. Here's Pam, Mr and Mrs O'Reilly. She's stocious drunk. Mind she doesn't throw up. Again. Oops. Sorry about that folks.'

'Sorcha, shut up,' said Pam, laughing, 'it wouldn't be like that. No way.'

'Not a chance. You get drunk, you carry yourself home to mammy and daddy.'

'You're a real pal.'

'Yes, I am. I'm protecting you,' said Sorcha.

'I bet Roger wouldn't drink,' said Pam slyly.

'You're right. He disapproves of all drugs, actually. So do,' Sorcha paused, about to say the Circle, checked herself and said instead, 'his friends.'

They joined the crowd. Both of them felt slightly unsure of how to behave. Neither of them were used to pubs, only going into them occasionally with their parents, mainly when on holidays.

One of the boys jumped up. 'Hiya girls. How did you do? I failed. You look great.' He looked at each of them in turn. Despite herself Sorcha was pleased, conscious of her freshly washed hair and newish jeans. She smiled. 'What'll you have?' Pam asked for a mineral. Sorcha said, 'Water please.' The boy, whom they did not know, said, 'Hey, what's with you two? Afraid of the big bad wolf? C'mon, have a real drink. It's much more fun.'

'No thanks, water will be fine for me,' said Sorcha. 'Yeh, sure. You must be a real drip.' He laughed. Pam said nothing.

While he went off to the bar they talked to the others about results. Some were quieter than others and Sorcha was not too keen to ask them, for fear of embarrassing them.

She saw the boy coming back. The place was so full that he had to weave sideways in and out of the people standing. The air was thick with cigarette smoke and full of chatter and singing, good-natured shouts and slagging. He arrived at the table. '- Name's Jerry, by the way. What's yours?' They told him. Sorcha could not see any water or mineral. 'This is mine,' he said, putting a pint of lager in front of him. 'And ... ' He took a bottle of cider from his jacket pocket and placed it in front of Pam along with a glass he'd been carrying, 'this is yours, Pam.' He looked directly at her. 'And for you, Sorcha, my next trick.' He took another, identical bottle from his other pocket. 'All yours,' he said as he placed it and the remaining glass in front of her. 'I forgot what you asked for. Sorry.' He looked at them both and smiled.

'I don't drink, Jerry,' said Sorcha.

'Don't mind her. She's a bit of a health freak,' said Pam, smiling at Jerry.

'I don't mind,' he said. 'It takes all kinds ... I respect your ideas.'

Sorcha was afraid that Pam would drink the cider and wanted to persuade her not to. 'Pam, come to the loo,' she ordered. Jerry smiled again. 'Girls always go to the loo together, the minute they come in. Discussing tactics, I reckon.'

In the toilet Sorcha said, 'Wow, he's a creep. "I respect your ideas",' she said, imitating Jerry's false sincerity.

'Yeh, but he's nice. And generous,' said Pam.

'C'mon, Pam, you know why he bought us that booze,' said Sorcha.

'No. Why ever did he do it, if it weren't for to slake our horrible thirsts, dahlin'?' Pam imitated a Southern Belle accent.

'Why, I jest think he might want his wicked way with one or t'other of us, honey pie,' answered Sorcha in the same style.

'Why, the dirty rat. I'll set our Daddy right on him, jest you see, dahlin',' simpered Pam and then, reverting to her ordinary voice said, 'He's cute though, isn't he?'

'I suppose so. But what about the cider? Don't drink it, Pam.'

'Leave me alone. I'll be OK. You have to start sometime.'

'No, you don't. That's the very point.'

Pam drank the cider and then drank Sorcha's one. She talked to Jerry most of the night. Sorcha joined in the singing and joking. Pam had a third cider, bought by Jerry. Sorcha leaned over to her. 'Careful, Pam, will you,' she said. 'I feel great,' said Pam.

By the time they were leaving, one of the boys in their group had started an argument with a man at the bar. It was just about to come to blows when the bouncer intervened and put the boy out. Everyone jeered him and after a minute he calmed down and shouted a few insults back through the door of the pub.

They walked along O'Connell Street singing and shouting. Gradually they broke into smaller groups. Some were going to a disco. Pam and Sorcha had to be back on the last bus at half eleven so they were going home.

Pam was linking Jerry's arm and they were deep in talk, laughing loudly and frequently. Sorcha went on to the bus stop. Finally, as the bus was coming Pam ran over. She turned and called, 'Bye, Jerry,' and stumbled, but quickly regained her balance.

On the bus she said, 'Ooh, I'm dizzy.' Sorcha noticed that she was not at all like they had been when pretending to be drunk on the way into town. She wondered would her parents notice and if they did what would they say. 'You'd better come to my house for tea,' she said, 'and we can phone your parents from there. You can stay, if they let you. They won't notice then.'

'Notice what?' said Pam, almost aggressively.

'That you're drunk.'

'I'm not drunk.'

'That you've been drinking then.'

Pam giggled. 'Ooh, I feel dizzy. Why is this bus spinning? Let's get another.'

'Pam, shut up.'

Pam's mother was not really surprised that she had gone to Sorcha's and allowed her to stay overnight. 'I suppose you only get your results once,' she said. They had tea in the kitchen and Nuala came in and joined them for a while. When she got Sorcha on her own for a minute she asked her had Pam been drinking.

'Well, we were in a pub but I don't think she had anything.' Sorcha didn't like lying but she didn't want to be the one to get Pam into trouble.

'Don't be stupid, Sorcha. It's obvious she's half skittered. Look at her, at her age. My God.'

'Hold on, mother. Have you never been drunk?'

'That's not the question here. Does Pam's mother know she drinks? Does her father? He'd kill her, I'm sure.'

'Hold on. She doesn't "drink", as you say it. She had a drink tonight, that's all. She won't do it again.'

'How do you know? Something has to be the start of it. I hope you weren't ...'

'No mother. I wasn't. In fact I tried to stop her. It's all the fault of this creep she met. She's seeing him again at the weekend, she says. He tried to get me to have one as well but I wouldn't. We Raffertys are made of stern stuff, my parent. Your daughter is safe.'

'I'm glad to hear that,' said Nuala, smiling. She put her arm around Sorcha's shoulder and hugged her briefly. 'Don't reason with Pam now, she won't listen, but talk to her tomorrow. Maybe I will myself. G'night, kid.'

'G'night, Mommy,' answered Sorcha in her John Wayne drawl.

* * *

Sorcha met Roger outside his house on Saturday night, as they had arranged. She'd had to tell Paul that there was an important meeting. She couldn't say she was going to a party with Roger. As it was Paul was far from pleased.

'Look, Sorcha, it's not that I mind the meetings, although I'm not saying I don't. There are too many of them, that's all. Well, that's part of it. But Saturday night is the only real night I can do anything. I'm always too knackered on Friday. And now this. It's the only time I ever see you.'

Leave school, then.' Sorcha saw his reaction. 'Joke. Honest. I'm sorry, really I am. But, really, this is important. It really is.' Sorcha was conscious of how often she was saying really when it was anything but.

'It always is. Really,' said Paul.

They finally parted on good terms, having had a quick cuddle and told each other how much they liked each other.

On the way to the house where the get-together was - Roger did not like to use the word party for this, it made it sound too frivolous - Sorcha told him about Pam and the drinking.

'Sorcha, if Pam drinks, ultimately that's her problem. You have some responsibility to try to stop her, I agree.' Here he looked hard at her. 'But as for yourself, don't. The Circle does not appreciate self abuse. We stand for a fresh world, cleansed of toxins and stupidity. Drugs, including alcohol, contaminate the individual. If we are contaminated, what possible hope would there be of us leading the inevitable change? Remember that.'

Sorcha felt the power of Roger's speech, power that came not just from himself but from the Circle and all it stood for. She was unsettled by that power. It made her feel as if she was inadequate, or could very easily become so, falling below the high standards required. She was glad that she had refused Jerry's cider.

The party was a quiet affair, very different from the gang's Great End of Summer Holiday Party. There were people sitting on chairs and on the floor, in groups, quietly and earnestly talking. There was no messing, no slagging, no high fashion, no make up. Sorcha instantly and easily thought of it as a 'get-together' and not a party. She was relieved to see that there was food, though, and mineral water and fruit juices. All the people that she imagined were in the Circle were there, Olivia, Brenda, Eoin, George and also Marian and Peter, whom she was not sure about. There were others as well. She recognised about half of them from various meetings but knew very few of their names.

After a few minutes George came over to her. Sorcha had never spoken to him on his own before. He had the same superior air that Roger had, the same distance and intensity, only much more pronounced. He gave a strong impression that there was no fooling with him, that he would have no time for small talk or teasing. Sorcha remembered the day in June when they had handed out leaflets and Simone had tried to come on to George. He had not been enthusiastic. She could see as he came over that he was making a point of talking to her. It suddenly occurred to her that George could be the boss of the Circle. She had, up to now, assumed that it was all very democratic or that if anyone was in charge it was Roger. Now she was not so sure.

'Hello, Sorcha.'

'Hi, George.' Sorcha swallowed, nervous with him. If she sometimes felt that Roger passed judgement on her and what she said, she knew this was different. The very reason George was talking to her was to size her up.

'So, it seems you've accepted our invitation.'

'That's right.' She knew he was waiting for her to speak so that he could examine her closely. She had no intention of making a fool of herself. She never liked it when Roger treated her like this and liked it less now with George, whom she hardly knew, especially now that she was part of the Circle.

'We're very pleased, you know,' he said.

'I should hope you are. You invited me, didn't you?' She wondered was she being too cheeky.

'It's serious, all of this. Well, you'll formally join at the meeting next week.' George walked off.

Sorcha felt that she had not gone down too well. 'Tough,' she said out loud, 'I don't like you either.'

She turned and saw Brenda smiling at her. Sorcha was glad to see her face, a welcome friend after George. She came over, her long straight hair flowing about her shoulders.

'Don't pay too much attention, he's a bit cross tonight,' said Brenda, taking Sorcha's arm and walking her across the room.

'He always seems like that.'

'It's just his personality. He wants you in. We all do. We all agreed. We're democratic, you know.'

Sorcha felt that she could be real friends with Brenda.

By this time a discussion had begun. Olivia was saying, 'Look, they'd obviously been planning it for ages. Any government would do the same to protect its own interests.'

'Now hold on.' A guy whom Sorcha did not recognise spoke. 'Let's be fair. Greenpeace have a lot of worldwide support. Most governments wouldn't back up what the French have done.'

'Look, the real problem is this.' Roger was speaking. Everyone turned to look at him. 'This is a serious issue. I got so angry when I heard it. The French government are treating the test site as if it's their property. But it's not. It's the world's property. They feel that people won't mind because public interest in the nuclear issue has faded, and it has to some extent since the end of the cold war. But the threat is still very much there. Look at the Gulf War. They talked for a while about using nuclear weapons against Iraq, remember. Greenpeace have a right, a duty to protest. We can't take this too seriously. It makes me so mad.'

'I agree with Roger,' said Eoin. 'They shouldn't be allowed to get away with this. It's the big arms companies that are behind it all. Each one of those warheads exploded means billions to them.'

Sorcha was amazed. Roger had told her to stay cool about this and now he was giving a lecture using all her ideas.

The discussion continued, voices breaking in from all angles.

'The only thing they'd understand would be a bomb.'

'Yeh. If we could get our hands on one I for one wouldn't hesitate. Right at the heart. Paris, or somewhere.'

'That's what some of the anarchist groups do. Boom. Wreck society 'cos it's so rotten. I can see their point.'

'The real thing is that they have good lawyers.'

'Of course they have. They'll get out. But it's too late. The warhead is exploded. Their right to protest has been taken away. Blow them up, that's what I say.'

Sorcha did not take part in any of this, she just listened. She was only mildly surprised. Often at the meetings speakers got swept up in their enthusiasm and suggested strange things. Someone once wanted to poison a reservoir for some reason. These ideas came like February snow storms, violent and intense, but melted away again, almost before they were over.

Later she said to Roger, 'So, you're into recycling ideas now?'

'What do you mean?'

'Well, the other day you made me throw out all my ideas and feelings about the Greenpeace thing. Then you recycled them and put them forward as your own, all bright and new. Even the anger I felt was there.'

For once Roger had nothing to say to Sorcha.

21

The sound of her heart thumping nearly blocked out Roger's words. 'We're having a special meeting tonight, as you all know. Sorcha is joining the Circle. We've watched Sorcha now for some months and we've seen her develop from a little schoolgirl who knew nothing to a committed adult who cares deeply about the most important issues facing this planet. We don't easily take in new members to the Circle but I think I can say that we're all very pleased to have her.' He sat down.

It crossed Sorcha's mind that George might not be as pleased as Roger. She had been nearly right about the members. Eoin, Brenda, Olivia, Roger and George - and Marian and Peter, whom she had suspected but not been sure of. There was another man as well, William, whom she had not known about. There were all there, sitting in a circle. And now Sorcha as well.

Earlier on Roger had rehearsed the ceremony with her. She knew what to do. It felt like her Confirmation all over again, except now she was on her own and once she joined the Circle it would change her life.

She stood up and stepped into the centre of the circle of chairs. Roger turned out the overhead light and that left Sorcha lit up by a single lamp, with the others around her in the gloom. She turned slowly, facing each of them in turn. Her palms were wet and her heart still pounded. George's voice came out of the shadow, reciting her vow, phrase by phrase, and she repeated it, solemnly, slowly turning.

'I am part of the Circle ... I willingly embrace ... its cause of saving the world ... I will work actively to this end ... I will keep everything of the Circle secret ... forever.'

Sorcha then raised her right hand and went to Brenda and extended her palm, fingers spread out. Brenda then raised her own left hand and they pressed their palms together, finger on finger and held them for a few seconds. As they were doing this Sorcha looked into Brenda's eyes and said, 'I swear.' Then she moved on and did the same with Eoin, Olivia, Marian, Peter, William, and then Roger. She would have stayed longer with him but could not read if there was anything special for her in his look. When she came to George she felt the coldness, first of his hand, then of his eyes. 'I swear,' she said and thought, he doesn't trust me. I'll prove he's wrong.

Roger turned on the centre light and everyone was smiling at Sorcha, congratulating her.

'Now, what do I need to know?' Sorcha asked brightly, all her nervousness gone. She could hardly believe it, that they had accepted her without doubt, without any reservations. She felt responsible and adult.

'At the moment the important thing is you understand just how we work,' said George.

'Yes,' said Brenda, 'the main thing is that we can't be found out. What we do wouldn't always ... meet the approval of others. No-one outside the Circle knows we exist. We meet very casually, in different houses or even in the open. We never have an agenda, or keep any records. We never talk about the Circle unnecessarily.

Olivia continued, 'We have the other meetings, the ones you've been coming to. They're, sort of, a cover, you know. Some of us come to them. Some don't. We can get things done that way. Without being found out, you know.' Her wavy hair half-covered her face. Sorcha didn't know what she was talking about.

Eoin took over, 'What Olivia is saying, Sorcha, is that all these other meetings are useful to us. They get people involved, raise their awareness. We get things done. They're also a cover. If anything was to happen, say a Garda investigation, let's be straight, there'd only be these big vague meetings organised by Roger.'

'Yes,' said Roger, 'everyone thinks I'm strange anyway. No one would ever guess we're all involved. See?'

'I see,' said Sorcha. She felt uneasy at the mention of the guards.

'That's why,' said George, 'you never, ever mention the Circle outside of a meeting. You never know who might be listening, do you?'

'I suppose not. Well, who's in charge?'

'The way it is, Sorcha,' said Brenda, 'we don't like that idea. That's the way society has been run all along, with someone in charge. We prefer to make decisions as a group. We all have our say.'

'I see,' said Sorcha again. Sorcha liked the idea of what Brenda was saying, but was not convinced that it was absolutely true. She had a feeling that there was more to the way the Circle was organised than that. She stayed on the lookout for a definite sign but saw nothing to back up her suspicion that someone was really calling the shots. The meeting went on, plans were made and finally they broke up.

'Till the next time,' everyone said, as they parted.

22

It was a dark night. The sky was clear and starry but there was no moon. The dim suburban street lights barely broke the blackness which seemed to suck all light into itself. Roger was standing on the pavement, hands in the pockets of his jacket, collar up. His breath clouded around his head. The nights had turned cold and it wouldn't be long before the mornings were frosty. He was waiting only a short time when a car pulled up. He opened the passenger door and slipped in. 'All set?' he asked.

Brenda was driving. 'The stuff's in the back.'

They said nothing else. They drove for a while and then she slowed down.

'Do you see him?' she asked.

'Yes, look, up ahead.'

She stopped the car and Eoin got in the back. 'All set?' he asked.

'The stuff's all there,' said Roger, 'in the back.'

They drove off. After a few minutes Roger said, 'Do you think she'll be all right?'

Brenda said, 'We'll see tonight. She's your little project, so she'd better be, or we're all in trouble.'

'Oh, she'll keep quiet, no matter what,' said Roger.

'It's a risk: we've taken it, so let's shut up about it,' said Eoin.

Sorcha was on the footpath, where they had arranged. She had got the bus from her house to the far side of the city, where the others were to pick her up. This was to make it more difficult for anyone to spot them. She climbed in beside Eoin. 'Hi,' she said.

'Everything's set,' said Roger. 'The stuff's in the back. We all know what to do.'

They drove back across the city and out towards Howth. There they parked the car in a car park used by couples and others who enjoyed the view of the city with the sweep of shimmering lights around the bay. The red lights on the masts on top of Three Rock were tiny gleaming eyes in the night-blackened mountains behind the south city. They said little, their conversation occasionally flickering to life and then going silent again. They were waiting until everything had shut down, so there would be few people about. Sorcha had told her parents that she was staying with a friend from school so that they would not get suspicious. The others did not need stories, as Roger came and went as he wanted to and Brenda and Eoin did not live at home.

After two hours they moved off. It was still too early, only one o'clock, but they did not want to arouse suspicion by staying too long in one place.

They drove around in silence. Once there was the siren of a Garda car and their faces inside the car were lit disconcertingly with the faint blue of its light, on and off, on and off as it came behind them. Sorcha twisted in her seat to look out the back window, sure that it was they the Guards were after.

'Turn around, will you,' snapped Eoin.

'It's the cops,' said Sorcha.

'Don't advertise yourself,' said Eoin.

Sorcha faced the front, looked again at Brenda's blue, dark, blue, dark head. The patrol car swept past them, turned a corner and faded quickly. 'I suppose I'm nervous,' Sorcha told the car. No one said anything. 'It's the first time I've done anything like this, you know.'

'Hey, try to relax. It's OK,' said Brenda, a trace of impatience in her voice. Sorcha was grateful to her for making some attempt to make her feel better, however small it was.

From time to time Sorcha wondered at the elaborateness of their plan. It had occurred to her that they could have skipped all the driving about but she held back each time she was going to mention it. They had said that this was a training mission, so she supposed there was some point to it.

Finally Roger said, 'It's time.' They were going to a chemist's shop on Fairview Strand, a wide straight road leading from the city towards Howth, bordered on one side by shops and on the other by the long, narrow Fairview Park. There were still cars along the road, their lights seeming to Sorcha to be aimed directly at her. The Park was pitch black. Sorcha peered across the road, trying to see if there was anyone in there. The darkness seemed filled with flitting, weaving shapes which she could easily imagine were hiding there especially to catch the four of them.

The chemist's shop was on a corner and Brenda turned the car into the side road and switched off the lights. They had chosen this shop because it sold a range of cosmetics which had been tested on live animals. Brenda had told her of the monkeys which had their eyelids pinned open while shampoos and conditioners had been dropped in their eyes, one drop to this monkey, two to that one. Others were shaved and creams rubbed into their skin in huge quantities over a long period. This was to measure the damaging effects of the products, to find the maximum amount of harmful substances they could use before being sued by an injured human customer. Brenda had said that there were cosmetics which were not tested on animals so this chemist had no excuse. Not that, she pointed out, they would be justified even if there was no alternative. Cosmetics, the Circle felt, were unnecessary and wasteful and distracted people from the true, simple life.

The plan was to daub slogans on the shop with paint, as a way of educating people and as a warning to other shops. They had agreed that the media did not pay attention to issues like this unless something unusual happened to attract their attention to them.

Sorcha had at first been shocked when, immediately after her initiation ceremony, the Circle had begun working out the plans for the attack. She had always assumed that when at the meetings this sort of thing was called for it was just hot air, people giving vent to strong feelings. Then suddenly she was actually planning action. She wondered had she let herself in for more than she had realised. She had not planned to do anything quite like this.

After the first few minutes of doubt she became engrossed in figuring out how to get the paint and brushes and the car and so on without attracting attention. It was exciting. She put her misgivings aside. She supposed that there was no point in the Circle and its secrecy if there was nothing worth hiding away, if it did what anyone else could do out in the open. She was fooling herself if she expected it to be otherwise.

At one point George had said, 'Are you worried about this, Sorcha? Have you doubts?'

She looked at him. 'No. I'm in. That's what the initiation meant, isn't it?'

As soon as the car stopped, Eoin and Roger slipped out. Roger quickly opened the boot and lifted out the cardboard box with the paint and brushes. He put it on the ground, took the screwdriver and quickly prised off the lids of the two cans of paint, one red, the other black. Eoin took a stick and stirred them rapidly. They each grabbed a can and a brush and walked to the shop front. Brenda stayed in the car, behind the wheel. Sorcha had walked to the main road and stood in the doorway of the neighbouring shop, eyes scanning the road and the footpaths. 'You've got about three minutes. There's a couple coming along the Strand,' she warned the others, without looking at them.

Roger and Eoin were painting. The Circle had decided, before Sorcha joined them, to use paint and brushes rather than spray cans. They believed that people using spray cans for this kind of work were lazy. It was another part of the laziness of the consumer society. They were harmful to the ozone layer and vandals and yobbos used them to write crude insults and 'Eric loves Sandra' on bus shelters. The Circle did not want to be confused with them in the public eye.

Eoin was painting PERFUME = TORTURE in red and Roger was working on TOWARDS A BETTER WORLD in black underneath it. The letters, each half a metre high dripped and slopped across the stone and glass of the shop front. The security shutter was inside the window, one of their reasons for choosing this shop. There would be little point in going to all this trouble if the owner raised the shutter in the morning and their work disappeared.

Sorcha was keeping an eye on the couple, who were walking slowly, stopping every now and then to kiss. There was not much danger from them until they were right alongside. Eoin was spelling out his letters 'T' and 'O' and the brushes slapped and dripped against the shop. Around the corner the engine of the car ran quietly. A few cars passed but none slowed. 'Hurry,' said Sorcha. They seemed to be taking for ever, although only a minute and a half had passed.

Without warning their ears were filled with the wail of a siren and blue lights lit the chemist's window and glistened on the paint. Sorcha was certain that the Gardaí were rushing from their hiding place in the Park. She froze in the doorway. Eoin spun around, a shout springing from his mouth, red paint spraying on the footpath and on the no parking pole. Roger's arm jerked, damaging the second 'T' in BETTER, the only one of his letters not perfect. It took less than a second for them to grasp that the explosion of activity was caused by an ambulance as it swung from the side road next to theirs into the main road. It careered off, tilting into the Malahide Road, heading for Beaumont Hospital.

Sorcha was shaking uncontrollably. She gasped, 'Oh no, oh no, oh no,' until Roger, who had gone back to his work said, without looking away from it, 'Take it easy, Sorcha, it's all right. Calm down.' Eoin was unable to stand still, jumping from foot to foot as he slapped the paint on even more vigorously and sloppily than before. 'It's OK, Sorcha. I'm dead as well. We're finished now. Let's go.' He finished the last 'E' and picked up his can. 'Wait. I'm not,' snapped Roger. He was on the 'W' of world. He had not increased his pace, annoyed enough with the damaged 'T', not wanting to make a mess. He did not want people to think that this had been done by slobs or amateurs.

Sorcha was regaining control. She checked the couple, who had stopped again but who were within half a minute of them if they walked at a regular pace. A car passed, a dark one. She thought there were two men in it but it was on the other side of the very wide road, heading for town, and she could not be sure. She kept an eye on it. As it came to the traffic island at the end of the Strand it slowed and indicated. The lights allowing it to leave by the exit lane were green but it did not slip off. The brake lights came on, went off, came on again. It was stopped now in the middle of the road.

'It's the cops,' shouted Sorcha. Instantly Roger and Eoin, who had been adding to his work to try to improve its appearance, picked up the cans and ran for the car. They were around the corner before Sorcha could move. She was alone in the doorway, the car was doing a u-turn, was now on her side of the road, coming back. She forced herself to act and leaped from her place. Her hair was held up in a knitted woollen cap and she was wearing dark clothes, as were all the others and she desparately hoped that these would make her invisible. The Garda car was not hurrying, so maybe they had not really seen what they were up to, were only being extra attentive to duty. As she rounded the corner Roger was straightening up from the boot, where he had replaced the box. His right hand was up, getting ready to slam down the lid. Eoin was disappearing into the car. As the boot lid came down she raced past Roger. 'They're coming,' she said. Brenda was moving before she or Roger had their doors shut. 'Hurry,' she shouted. 'Shut up,' said Roger, tense but calm. There was a junction about fifty metres along, with a choice of two directions. Brenda took the left, as they had arranged. Eoin and Sorcha were both half turned so that they faced each other but their heads were twisted right back to the rear windscreen. As they swung around the corner they could see the front of the Garda car. They both thought they saw the flash of a blue light. 'Did they see us?' asked Roger still calm, still tense. 'Hard to say,' said Eoin. 'I don't know, I'm sure they did,' said Sorcha. She was in danger of panicking. Oh no, she said to herself, why? why?

The area they were in was criss-crossed with roads, like a rabbit warren. 'Designed for eluding followers,' Roger had said at the meeting. It was another one of the reasons for choosing that shop. The car lurched to the right. Neither Eoin nor Sorcha saw any sign of the following Garda car. Then it was a series of turns and racing forward, far too fast and braking hard for the next one, then left, then right. This area was bounded by Fairview Strand on one side and wide, straight Griffith Avenue on the other. They had, in their plan, figured that they could probably lose a following car but that the Gardaí would most likely head for Griffith Avenue when it became clear they had lost them. It would be easy to stop the few cars that would come out at this hour until they got the right one. Brenda turned on to Phillipsburgh Avenue and headed back to Fairview Strand. They turned for town, sorry that they could not go back past the chemist's to see their work. 'Blasted cops,' said Roger. He sounded more angry at them for interrupting than relieved that they had escaped.

Sorcha was staying the little of the night that was left in Roger's house. He made up a bed for her downstairs and as he was going up to his room he stood at the doorway. 'Are you OK now?' he asked.

'Yes, thanks. Wow, I really got scared out there for a while. But you know what, it was exciting as well. What would I have done if I'd been caught?' Then she felt like a little girl again. She felt ill suddenly, from fear. She imagined her parents shocked and hurt and enraged. A shadowy image of the Smiths began flickering in front of her. She shook it off. The moment passed. She was responsible for herself. 'Yes, it was exciting, wasn't it?'

Roger smiled at her, his earlier irritation gone. 'Do you know, I only got 'WOR' of WORLD done? What on earth will they think of us?'

23

'What about your homework?' came Eoin's predictable complaint from the sitting room.

'I'll do it later, don't worry,' answered Sorcha and pushed Paul out the door and quickly followed him, pulling it closed after them. 'Let's go before he gets awkward.'

Paul had been trying to answer a physics question and had got hopelessly bogged down so he decided that a walk was the only way to clear his head. He had been going to go on his own but at the last moment called for Sorcha instead. He had been reluctant, not sure how they would get on but was glad when she answered the door and jumped at his suggestion, and nearly at him.

'Where to, Madam?' he asked as Sorcha linked his arm.

Sorcha had had no plan up to that moment but suddenly had an idea. 'Long or short, Sir?' He decreed long so she said, 'To the sea, so.' To get to the sea they would pass Fairview Strand and the chemist's shop. Sorcha had an urge to see the result of the previous night's work.

'You look as if you haven't slept a wink,' said Paul.

'I was over in Eileen's last night, working on a project, you know.' Sorcha could not help noticing how one lie always led to another. She pacified her conscience by telling herself that it was in a good cause and that it would be idiotic, and unfaithful, to go telling Paul about her adventure.

'Who's Eileen? Never heard of her before.'

'No, probably not. We were put to work on it by the teacher. Silly old thing. It's on the Reformation. For history, you know.'

'Do you still do projects? We gave them up years ago.'

'So did we. Until this one.' Sorcha was anxious not to continue, in case Paul became suspicious. 'Do you know what vivisection is?' she asked.

'No, but I suppose you'll tell me.'

She realised that this was not a good topic either, under the circumstances, so she said, 'OK I won't.'

'Hey, don't get touchy. It's to do with animals, isn't it?' placated Paul.

'Oh, Paul, it's horrible. The things they do, just for money. They even cut the tops off the heads of cats and stick electrodes in their brains, just to watch the reaction. I can't help thinking of Trixie.' Trixie was Sorcha's cat of many years, a marmalady type who owned the house and never gave anything in return, least of all affection. For all that Sorcha loved her.

'I can think of a few people I wouldn't mind doing that to. Some of my teachers, for instance. Stick one in there,' Paul mimed pushing an electrode viciously into a head, 'and watch old Brennan squirm. Another in there and turn Paddy Haugh into a gibbering idiot, if only he wasn't one already.'

'Or Jeff, and put him off girls,' joined in Sorcha.

'Or Molly and give her an idea.'

'Or you and make you kiss me.'

Paul threw his arms up, grabbed his head and howled, 'It's working, it's working.'

Sorcha could feel his lips still laughing as they touched hers. Afterwards he said, 'Or Roger and turn him into a biodegradable rubbish bag.'

Sorcha stopped short. 'Are you still jealous?'

'Yes, I am actually.'

She said nothing and they walked on in silence for a time. He had said before that he was jealous but she could sense that this time it was really serious and hurtful for him. She wanted to tell him that there was no need to feel that way. She did not want to be untrue about it, though. What would be the point anyway? If she misled him and told him lies about how Roger was insignificant in her life Paul would only think that she cared more for Paul himself than she actually did, and she was not really sure how deep were her feelings for him any longer. She wanted to think that for Roger she felt respect and nothing more. Yet, she remembered the night she kissed him.

Paul was waiting, scared of what she would say. Somewhere inside a claw gripped him. His mouth dried up. It did not seem right to him that she spent so much time with Roger and the others. She was supposed to be going with him, to be his girlfriend. That meant that he was the special one. With Sorcha that didn't seem to be the way. Yet he loved her. He had thought he fancied Pam for a while but after the party he realised how much he really liked Sorcha. He had hardly seen her because of study and often became distracted, thinking about her. Most of his books and copies had her name in carefully printed lettering on them. She was the real reason why he had to give up on his physics question and get out of the house. He constantly wondered whether she was with Roger while he was at home with his books.

He looked at her as they walked. She was deep in thought, her face beautiful in its profile, the breeze blowing her hair around her mouth and eyes now and then. He was very conscious of having kissed that mouth only a few moments before and didn't want to lose her. 'Hey,' he began and she turned to look at him, questioning with her eyes. 'Hey,' he said again. He was going to say it was all right, forget about jealousy and Roger, let's just go on as we were, but he could not. He could not rest as it was. He had to know one way or the other. Roger or him. He looked at her. She still said nothing.

Finally she looked as if she was going to speak. Paul was miserable, yet hope was there, waiting to break loose if she said the right word, and flow over him and lift him high.

'Look, Paul, it's not that simple.' Nothing, thought Paul, let down, ever is with you, Sorcha. 'You say you're jealous. What do you want of me? Am I to give up everything that's become important to me? Just because you're jealous?'

Paul didn't feel like it but thought he had better say something. 'It's not that. I just ... '

'I know. You're afraid that I don't love you.'

'Yes.'

'But it's also that you want me to be different. You probably wouldn't love me then anyway, even if I was.'

They walked on. Neither felt that this was getting anywhere. Paul didn't feel any better or any more secure. Sorcha still was not sure what she wanted to say, or how to say it.

'It's that, if you're my girlfriend you're supposed to be special. As it is you run off the whole time with those others,' he paused, 'and with Roger.'

'No. What you mean, Paul, is that if I'm your girlfriend you're supposed to be special. And you are. Really you are.'

'Why doesn't it feel like that then?'

'You'll have to accept me as I am, then you'll feel better.'

Paul still was not happy. She had said nothing, really, about Roger, so he asked her directly what she felt about him.

Sorcha could feel herself holding back. 'I told you before, it's all to do with this group. Nothing more. That's a promise.'

It still wasn't great but it seemed the best they could do and Paul somehow sensed that this was all he was going to get, and resigned himself to it. A reduced Sorcha was better than no Sorcha. Sorcha felt she had not been completely honest but she really didn't know how to be any more so. She didn't want to hurt Paul, and sensed that to be any more open would be to put herself in too vulnerable a place. At least part of the reason she stalled was to protect herself.

She leaned against Paul as they walked and he put his arm around her shoulders. She put hers around his waist. They walked in silence and gradually a calmness grew between them. They were both comfortable with it and it seemed to fit them for that time.

As they came into Fairview Sorcha disentangled herself. It was getting dark. She hoped that they would be able to see the writing clearly. Of course it could have been cleaned up by then. She looked at the shop. There in red sloppy letters was PER-FUME = TORTURE, perfectly legible but even messier as a result of Eoin's botched attempts to fix it up when he was waiting for Roger to finish his painting. Below it, in neat black square capitals sat, as awkward as a half-dressed public speaker, TO-WARDS A BETTER WOR. She slowed down, images of the night before, the slap of the hurried paintbrushes, the flashing light, the lurching car taking over her attention. Her shout of warning was again in her ears when Paul said, 'Hey, look at that. What's it about? I know. It's the vivisection stuff you were talking about earlier. Were your crowd involved? Did you do this, Sorcha in the dead of night, under cover of a blanket of darkness?'

She thought again of last night and the dark of the park opposite, now losing its shape in the dimming light, the trees blackening against the purply blue of the sky. It had been unsettling then and, in a rush, she was unsettled again. She wondered momentarily was Paul really joking or did he suspect. She knew, though, that he would not, that it would never seri-ously occur to him.

'Yes, I confess. It was me. I came here in a car and did this, unknown to anyone save my few dozen closest companions,' confessed Sorcha a in mock-serious tone, matching his.

'What's a BETTER WOR?' Paul joked.

'Uh, I ... it's,' she thought of Roger and his perfect letters that still failed to communicate. She smiled and went on. 'It's a machine for testing cosmetics. You put them in the WOR and it analyses them and tells you what animals have been used in their manufacture.'

At that moment a Garda on foot patrol came around the corner. Paul called, 'Garda, here's the culprit. I've apprehended her for you, the nasty little anarchist.'

The Garda looked at them, decided that they were not serious and grinned, walking by.

Sorcha could feel herself blushing fiercely. She could not return the smile and kept her face lowered. Paul noticed and said,

'Ha! A guilty conscience.' He turned after the Garda. 'Guard, Guard,' he called.

Sorcha thumped him as hard as she could between the shoulder blades. It had the desired effect. He stumbled forward, unable to speak. 'Shut up, you swine,' she said, her eye on the Garda, who kept to her slow patrol pace and did not turn around.

Paul recovered, gasping, 'I'll kill you.' Sorcha fled and he gave chase.

* * *

Later on in the week, at dinner, Nuala said, 'Did you see that report in the paper, Eoin, about all those shops being daubed?'

Sorcha's heart lurched and began to pound at a frantic pace, as it had done several times recently.

Her father said, 'No, what's it about?'

'It seems that four or five shops, mainly chemists, were daubed earlier in the week with anti-vivisection slogans. The Guards think it's one of those fanatical animal rights groups. You know the sort, Sorcha, who prefer animals to humans.'

Sorcha wondered did her mother suspect, or was she trying simply to involve her in the conversation.

'Well it's not me. We're not animal rights, although we do believe that people treat animals terribly.'

'I wasn't suggesting for a moment it was you,' said Nuala, 'but these groups can get carried away, you must admit.'

'Look, it's not as if a bit of paint is that awful,' Sorcha defended.

'No,' said Eoin, 'I agree. What they do to animals is grotesque. Not that I'm approving of breaking the law. But there's no need to sell stuff like that. Protests might make them sit up and take notice.'

'Right, Dad. When there's money in it nothing else will make them think. If people see the protests they might stop buying the gunge and then we'll - they'll have won, I mean.' If either of her parents noticed her slip they did not say.

'Right,' said Eoin. 'It's not like doing something awful, like poisoning a reservoir or anything.'

'OK,' said Nuala. 'We'll add cosmetics to our boycott list right away.'

Sorcha laughed. Neither she nor her mother ever used any cosmetics.

When dinner was over Sorcha had time to think about what her mother had been saying. She was puzzled. There had been no mention of more that one daubing at the meeting. Unless there was another group, which seemed an unlikely coincidence, the members of the Circle had not been fully open with her.

She got a chance, later on, to slip around to Roger. 'What's going on?' she asked, as soon as he came to the door. He said he did not know what she was talking about. She told him about the reports.

'Sorcha, you're new. We had to break you in gently, to get you used to things gradually.'

'To see if you can trust me, more likely. I thought that if I'm in the Circle, I'm in. I didn't know I was half a member.'

'Sorcha, you're a member, like everyone else. Just don't get too nosy. You don't understand everything, not yet. Be cautious.'

Sorcha did not like the warning tone of Roger's remarks. She wondered again what was going on. She thought of her father's comment on poisoning reservoirs and remembered talk like that at meetings, and talk even of bombs. She wanted to be sure that she knew what they were doing, if it was in her name.

But she also remembered why she was in the Circle, what was happening in the world. Roger had said you must fight fire with fire. He was right. If they had gone into the chemists' and asked them all to stop selling and supporting the offensive products would they have said, 'Yes, certainly.' Not a chance, thought Sorcha. Now, though, if the public only listened, they just might be forced to comply. So a slightly illegal act could have very good results. An even bigger act, on a more serious issue, could produce even better results. Sorcha decided not to judge these things until she knew all of the facts, all of the reasons behind them.

24

'Look at him,' said Pam, 'he's solid hunk.'

'Mmm,' agreed Sorcha, 'not bad. I'd say his brains are on the bicycle seat, though.'

'Oh, you're never satisfied, Sorcha. Always complaining about something.'

'Hey, hold on. I'm not complaining. I just made an observation about the likely site of the chap's thinking apparatus. He looks as if he uses it to sit with, that's all.'

'He's just a guy. It's OK for you, you've got someone.' Pam could not bring herself to say Paul's name. Up until the Great End of Summer Holiday Party she had felt that she was doing well with him. Then he had gone off with Sorcha again. As far as she could make out they had seen each other a good bit since, even though Paul was supposed to be stuck in the house every night, studying. She had phoned him and he had been friendly but Pam felt it was friendly like the way the people in the shops sometimes were - not very sincere. He had said he couldn't go out because he was up to his neck in work. Yet when she asked Sorcha, casually, in school a few times how he was Sorcha always seemed to have seen him the night before.

'What about Jerry?' asked Sorcha.

'Oh, him.' Pam threw her eyes up to heaven. 'I didn't tell you. He's a creep. The usual. After the one thing. We went out a few times, as you know.'

'Yeh. I thought it was going OK though.'

'The first once or twice wasn't so bad. By the third time we'd gone to the pub and the pictures three times and I'd been groped three times. The jokes were the same. Recycled rubbish.'

'Well, I hate to tell you that I told you so.'

'I know, I know. Hey, want to go for a drink tonight?'

'For a drink?'

'Yeh, a drink. You're in danger, Sorcha Rafferty, of becoming a first class bore. Bore grade one.'

'I'm not going to drink, and I don't think you should, Pam.'

'Little goody two shoes. Tell everyone what they should do. Save the world.'

'Well, someone has to do it. If it's not me, who'll it be? See?'

Pam smiled, but wondered if Sorcha was half joking, all in earnest, as her mother liked to say.

'Well, are you coming or not tonight?'

'I've got a meeting. I can't.'

'Another meeting. What on earth do you do?'

'Oh, discuss things. We're planning a few protests for the Christmas shopping period. Like the leaflets in the summer.'

The icy cold wind blew then, and they both remembered those long, dry, sunny days. Now the trees were nearly all bare, the evenings were very short, the mornings frosty. It had rained, on and off, for much of the past week. Suddenly Sorcha did not feel like going out. The fire and the TV seemed much more attractive.

When eight o'clock came she had put these thoughts out of her mind. She upbraided herself with the teaching that if you were serious about something you had to expect a little bit of inconvenience. The meeting was in Brenda's flat, and as usual she walked with Roger. It was acceptable to use a car for the cause but not for ordinary life. She noticed that he seemed tensed up. He didn't look at her the way he usually did and more than once didn't seem to hear what she said to him.

Brenda hugged Sorcha as soon as she opened the door. 'Good to see you.' As usual Sorcha was pleased. She felt that Brenda was sincere, that at least she was not using her, or not being not open with her. She seemed so glad that Sorcha had joined the

Circle. 'Another woman,' she had said, 'We need to get some balance into this group.'

They sat in their usual circle. No one said anything at first. Then Eoin gave a report on the Fairview message painting. He said that it had gone well except for the Gardaí and Brenda told them that they would probably have been caught if it wasn't for Sorcha's good work, keeping watch. They were all pleased with her, even George.

There was another silence which Sorcha broke, saying, 'I wanted to ask something.' All the heads turned to her. 'Were there other messages? I mean, were we the only ones, that night?'

'Yes, there were, in fact,' said George, his tone cool.

'But, I didn't ...,' Sorcha paused. 'None of that was discussed at the last ... meeting.'

'Did you not know? Well I told you, we only know what we need to know,' said George, confusingly.

'But ... when was it planned? ... When were the plans made?'

'What are you getting at?' George sounded irritated. Sorcha decided to drop it and said nothing more.

'For ages now it's been annoying me,' began Brenda. 'One of the big companies, Panrab, has this policy of producing food in Third World countries. Cereals and so on, for baby food. They use the most appalling pesticides.'

'Even DDT, which was banned in the West years ago. Their workers haven't even been told of the danger. They don't even wear protective suits,' George added.

'But that's not all. They've been involved in clearing the rain forests to get cheap land to grow this stuff. The lungs of the earth, the very lungs are being destroyed,' Brenda said.

'It's the same, the same story,' said Roger. 'They're like the others. They want everything now. Now. To hell with tomorrow.'

'All of the mainstream groups have protested, looked for bans on their products but have got nowhere. It's not popular enough in the media.'

'You've all seen their advertisements,' said George. 'They've a few different brands of baby food. The ideal family scenes.

Everything lovely. "For your baby's future," they say, "Because you care, we care" and stuff like that. It makes me sick.'

'All they think about is profit.' Brenda was standing up. Her voice was hard, like polished metal. When her look paused on Sorcha on its circuit of the group she seemed to hang there a little longer than on anyone else. Sorcha could not look away. She could see fields at the edge of magnificent, dense, mysterious forest, home to millions of animals, birds so strange, wide, sluggish yellow rivers, crystal clear waterfalls tumbling out of dense, rock-strewn greenery into deep pools, exotic tribes. She could see the massive yellow machinery used to drag the felled trees away, the cleared barren boundary-less fields, smell the air still heavy with the scent of newly-cut wood. Over it all was the mist of the chemical spray, the peasant workers with the bottles on their backs, inhaling the slow death. Later the harvest would come, the produce would go to the factory, the bottles of processed food with their cute labels to the supermarket shelves. Still later the new fields, overfarmed and chemically saturated would become barren and would be abandoned to their desertion for new acres hacked out of the forest.

Emotion mixed and boiled in her. Words churned in the seething cauldron of her insides. She felt like she had the day she fought with Conor, only this time there was a reason and a real enemy to turn on.

'It's evil. It's the worst thing. The very worst thing,' was what she said.

Such was the power in her voice, that the others all turned to her, even George, with a new respect.

'What we have to do,' said George, 'is hit them where it hurts.' He swept through them with his look. 'In their pockets.'

'We must hit sales,' said Brenda, almost shouting. 'Sales. Money. We must make it impossible for them to sell.'

Silence followed. Then Sorcha asked, 'How?' She was almost afraid of what the answer would be.

'Get to the source,' said George. 'The baby food.'

'It stands to reason,' Brenda broke the silence, 'if no one will buy the baby food, they'll be forced to change their tactics.'

'You're right. You're so right,' said Eoin quietly. 'You've got the right idea, that's for sure.'

'So, what do we do?' asked Sorcha, tension making her voice unsteady.

'It's not that simple. We can't do it easily,' said George, 'we'll have to think carefully.'

'True,' said Eoin, 'you're right. We'll have to think. Carefully. That's for sure.' He, like Sorcha, was obviously tense, his voice shaking.

'These people can't be allowed to go on. They're faceless. No one knows who they are.' Brenda's voice was on the point of losing control, but never quite beyond it.

'So, what do we do?' Sorcha asked again.

'We'll have to work together. More than ever before, we all have to stick together on this one.' George's voice was level, his gaze like Brenda's sweeping around the circle. 'Does everyone agree? Are we in this totally?' He looked longer at Sorcha than at the others. 'Are we?'

Eoin said, 'You're right, George. This is the serious one. We'll have to be in this together, up to the hilt. This isn't like the others, that's for sure.'

Eoin had begun to irritate Sorcha. She looked at him. She had not noticed before that he was quite so imbecilic. 'So what do we do?' This time Sorcha allowed impatience to escape into her voice.

Brenda finally said, 'I'm for getting at the baby food. In the supermarkets. Contaminate it. That'll make people sit up and take notice.'

No one said anything. Sorcha realised she had been waiting for this. Brenda could not have been thinking of anything else. Her mind raced with the implications of it. First she was terrified, then thoughtful.

'Contaminate it.' Eoin broke the short silence. 'Wow. That's serious. That's new, that's for sure.' He seemed taken aback by the idea.

'You're right,' Roger said, emphatically. 'Nothing else will impress them. We've tried to get the media interested before with no success. If we do this they won't be able to keep away.'

'I don't know,' said Olivia quietly. 'It's against the law.'

'Daubing walls is against the law,' said George. 'So is sending threatening letters, and you've done that.' He was intense in his look towards her, his voice quietly menacing. Olivia was silenced.

Marian said, 'But the babies. They didn't do anything.'

'We're not after the babies.' Again George's voice was unpleasant.

'It's the parents. We'll let everyone know. No one will buy the stuff. They'll have to withdraw it,' Roger spoke.

'No one will get hurt. If they do, it'll be Panrab's fault. We'll warn them,' said Brenda.

George, Brenda, Roger. They looked at everyone. There was something about them. It struck Sorcha with a jolt that they had planned this before the meeting. There was not only the Circle then. There was something else, smaller, even more secret. She wanted to be in it. She wanted to be a part of it all, of everything.

'We've got to do it,' she said slowly. 'Risks, personal sacrifices are necessary. That's what the Circle is for. We need results.' She looked at the three in turn, then quickly at the others.

Misgivings were eventually quietened. Peter's father was a doctor and he agreed to steal some poison. He said he could do it with no trouble. William was going to draft a letter to send to Panrab and to the papers. He said that he'd cut the letters out of newspapers. George didn't seem impressed with that and warned him not to leave any trace around his house. Roger was the one who was actually going to do the contaminating. Olivia would buy some baby food. Roger would fix it up and slip it back on the shelves in various supermarkets in the city. Sorcha had nothing to do directly but would be on hand in case any of the others needed her. They were not to meet again until after it was over.

On the way home she asked Roger about other meetings, an inner circle, as she named it to herself.

'What? George, Brenda, me meeting? When Sorcha? What for? We're all part of the Circle, aren't we?'

Sorcha was not convinced.

After she left Roger she walked on home on her own. She was light, airy, lifted. She had committed herself in a way that would have been unimaginable a short while ago. This time they really would stop totally horrible things. They would have an effect. And no-one would be hurt. The threat would be enough. And she might get nearer the inner circle if she did the right things.

Her mother commented on her good humour before she went to bed.

25

The waiting was the worst part. Each day dragged on interminably. Each morning she woke to anxiety. The normal routine had to be observed. Shower, breakfast, the radio. She had to listen to the eight o'clock news as if it was the same as always, through the crunch of toast and the occasional talk. All the time her whole body felt like a receiver, waiting for word of it to be beamed from the transmitter. There was never anything. At first she knew, despite her tension, that it was too soon for it to have been done. Later, each day was potentially the one, and still there was nothing. School brought no release. Classes passed miserably slowly, teachers' voices droning on and on. The bad weather continued and the school was filled with the smell of damp coats, the windows were runny and steamy. More than once she was asked, exasperatedly, what was wrong with her. The evening news was worse, if anything, than the morning one. Still, there was nothing. Either Roger had not done it yet, or William's message had been ignored. She did not know which would be worse. If they did ignore the warning it would only be a matter of time before some poor baby was poisoned. If that happened it would be their fault, not the Circle's. It was up to them to take action.

She couldn't contact Roger because they had agreed that there would be no contacts between the members for fear of arousing suspicion. So the evenings dragged on, homework half-done, television half-watched until bed time. Then it was disturbed sleep and anxious dreams until the next morning.

She had no interest in phoning Paul. She knew she'd have nothing to say to him. When he finally contacted her it was as she had feared it might be. They had been talking for a while when he said, 'Hey, you didn't ask me how the study was going.'

'How's the study going?' Sorcha could hear that her voice was flat.

'Hey, don't kill yourself with interest.'

'Sorry, Paul. I'm just distracted. What the hell's the point of it all?'

'Don't tell me you're at that again. Why don't you leave off? You're nicer then.'

'No, I'm really asking, not giving out. What's the point? I'm not staying in school any more. I'm getting out.'

'Oh, come off it, Sorcha. Look, I've got to study. Give me a break, will you.'

Later she said it to her parents.

'You, I hope, are making a joke of some kind,' said Eoin. Sorcha could see that he was not at all sure.

'No, I'm serious, Dad. I've no intention of becoming part of this whole silly business. And if I'm no ...'

'Now, hold on, at least for a minute. Talk about this slowly.' He sounded now as if he knew she wasn't making fun. 'Tell me what's the problem.'

'No problem. I'm leaving school. There's no point in staying.' Sorcha knew that she was being aggressive and knew that wasn't going to help her case, yet she seemed unable to stop herself.

Nuala came in and said, 'What's up?' No one said anything for a moment and then Eoin told her.

'I see,' said Nuala calmly. 'Are you serious about this, or are we having a little joke?'

'Serious,' said Eoin, 'I think.'

'Yes, I'm bloody well serious. I'm not a stupid kid. Don't speak to me like this. I won't have it,' exploded Sorcha.

'Hold on, now. Wait a minute. Go slowly and tell us what's actually the problem,' Nuala said, still patient.

Not for the first time Sorcha was struck by how much they were in agreement at times like this. Even the words they used were the same. They seemed to have an instinct for it.

'The problem is, I'm sick of it. Sick.'

'Sick of what, actually?' asked her mother, still in her reasonable tone.

'Sick of it all, actually.' Even through her anger Sorcha knew that they deserved more than this and that they would demand it.

'Sick, if you could be a little more precise, of what exact "it"?' asked Eoin, trying to be as patient as Nuala seemed to be and not making a very good job of it. He was finding Sorcha and her combination of being off-hand and angry extremely annoying.

'Everything. "It" means everything. The whole lot. I'm not going to work in those stupid companies, exploiting people. So there's no need ... '

'What companies? What work?' Nuala asked, exasperation at last creeping in to her voice.

'If I'm an engineer or anything else, I'll have to be part of the whole exploitation of the environment, the people ... '

'Ah, so that's what this is all about. It's Roger and that silly group. I suspected as ... '

Sorcha wanted to scream and run but she still knew that they deserved an explanation. If she was responsible for her life, for the world, she could not run away screaming from everyone who was being stupid or predictable and defensive. She interrupted her father.

'Don't start that. Roger did not tell me anything. I've got my own mind. I am not going to be a part of this system so there's no point ...'

'Of course Roger ...' interrupted Nuala.

'Will you listen,' shouted Sorcha. They stilled, with obvious effort, and she went on. 'There's no point in staying and doing the Leaving if I'm not going to do any of those jobs. That's it. I want to leave now and sort out my life.'

She knew they would not agree and was happy enough in the end when they did not lay down the law but said that they would discuss it with her again after the Christmas exams, which Sorcha knew she was going to mess up if she kept up her present rate of study. That might be to her advantage, she knew, as they might see it her way if she was doing badly.

Nuala and Eoin had decided that it was better to ease off on her, guessing that it would only make her more angry if they kept insisting that she stay on in school. What they did not realise was that this was not just a passing fancy of Sorcha's but that her whole life and view of the world had genuinely changed since the summer. She was perfectly sincere in wanting to leave school and had every intention of doing so as soon as possible.

* * *

When Saturday night came Sorcha really did not want to see Paul. In her mind he was completely of the world that she was turning her back on. He wanted to get on, wanted to have a nice easy life. She had wavered for a long time swinging backwards and forwards, between two worlds, between her parents, Paul, study, success, predictability, and in the end of it irresponsibility, and Roger and the Circle and full awareness of the world and its problems and full responsibility for her part in it. Lately she had swung towards the latter way and stayed there, like a pendulum whose mechanism had jammed, leaving it rigid and raised from the centre, at the top of its swinging arc. Everything from the other side was now outside her world and no longer interesting to her.

Paul phoned her and she agreed to go out with him. She was irritable the whole time and the tension they had felt on the phone earlier in the week hung between them like a mist, making them cold and distant with each other. They were both glad when they could quickly kiss each other goodnight and go home. Paul was particularly annoyed as he thought about it afterwards. He was working incredibly hard and he felt he deserved to relax and have some fun when he did go out, and that Sorcha certainly was not helping him, she was so caught up in her own ideas.

His birthday was during the week but he still did not want to come out. Sorcha bought him a huge card, her enthusiasm falling far short of the intensity the card supposed, and a present. She brought these around to him and stayed talking for half an hour or so. It turned out that he was surprised and pleased and they were relaxed and enjoyed each other's company. Then Paul went back to his study.

Finally Sorcha met Roger. She was able to call to his house during the week, the second since the meeting. No one could possibly be suspicious of that.

'Any progress?' she asked. They were walking along the streets near Roger's house. He did not want to talk about it, in order to make sure that secrecy was maintained.

'Aren't we being a little too cautious?' said Sorcha archly. 'Just a teeny bit? We don't think anyone would be listening to us out here, do we?'

'This is a serious business, Sorcha. Don't mock it. You really can't tell when you give something away. That's how people get caught. Afterwards.'

She was going to make a joke but caught his mood from his manner. He was looking about him and his voice was low and very serious.

Suddenly he said, talking quickly, almost breathlessly, 'I've got the stuff, the bottles. All I have to do is wait for the last few details to fall into place. I'm expecting that any day now. Then I get to work. It could be all over by the weekend after next.'

Sorcha was impressed. 'Where have you hidden it?'

Roger was aghast. 'Don't be stupid. How could you even ask that? It's safe.'

'Is the letter ready?' asked Sorcha, more carefully.

'How do I know? We don't keep in daily contact about it. That's the whole point.'

'But you have everything else, yes?'

Roger's glance was darting everywhere at once. He did not answer.

'Yes?' prompted Sorcha.

'Well not everything. I told you. I've got the bottles.'

Sorcha realised that all he had got were the bottles of baby food. Peter had not turned up with the poison, the essential thing, yet.

'Roger, you dolt. Anyone could have bought baby food. That's nothing.' It was the first time that Sorcha had spoken to Roger in that tone, mocking and familiar, as an equal.

He was not amused. 'Don't speak like that. Careless talk causes trouble. People could get caught. We have to hit these people where it hurts. Where it hurts badly. There is no time for joking now. There is no time for being lax,' Roger's voice was rising in volume with each word he spoke.

'Shh, you'll be heard,' Sorcha cautioned, unable to resist a further chance of making fun of him. They had arrived back at Roger's house and he went straight in. 'Don't contact me again until this is over. I'll phone you if I need you.'

Sorcha surprised herself by sticking out her tongue at his earnest back as it intensely made its way up his path, past the potato ridges, to the hall door.

On the way home she thought about him. Really in ways he was not very nice. He intimidated people the way he looked at them. He had hi-jacked her ideas. She really felt that she could only half trust him. And he was so serious about everything.

Still, he was in the inner circle, she was sure, and she wanted to be there as well.

***

Roger, Brenda and George were discussing Sorcha. They had met specifically to do so. It had been Roger's idea, after she had called to him. He was worried about her attitude.

'It was your idea to have her in. I was never keen,' said George.

'Look, what's the point in throwing up that sort of recrimination? She's in.' answered Roger.

'He's right,' said Brenda. 'She's in. Like it or not she knows about what's going on. The question is what do we do now.'

'What exactly did she say, that has you so worried?' asked George thoughtfully.

'It's not so much what she said, it's her attitude. She seemed to be light-hearted about the whole thing.'

'That's not a crime,' said Brenda.

'No-one says it is,' George snapped at her. 'We have to protect ourselves.'

'Look, I only called you because we agreed to report anything that could compromise us.'

'You were right to. If we're seriously undermined we'll have to call it off. We agreed on that,' said George darkly.

'Roger, is she really unsafe?' asked Brenda.

'No. I actually don't think so. I'm just following our plan, being cautious.'

'See. No problem. Is there?' Brenda always sounded satisfied like that but Roger had often seen her rear up suddenly when everyone thought she was placid and unconcerned.

'There'd better not be a problem. We've gone too far here. Even what we've done so far is a serious crime.'

'George, there's no problem. She was just a bit flippant, that's all. She was making fun,' said Roger.

'Of what?' asked Brenda.

'Of me, actually. She said that I was being too cautious.'

'I hope you told her that carelessness can get people into trouble,' said George.

'Yes, I did.'

'I've let her know before that I'm uneasy about her. Roger if you were wrong about her ...'

'I'm not. She's OK. If I am wrong I'll be the first to make sure that she's not let away with it.'

'Are you sure about that?' asked Brenda, very earnestly now. It was as if she was boxing Roger, having manoeuvred him into a corner.

'I've done it before, I'll do it again.'

'But it's different this time, isn't it?'

'What the hell do you mean?' Roger was angry now.

'You like her, don't you?' Brenda said pointedly.

'So what if I do? You know that personal issues aren't allowed to get in the way with us. I hope you're not trying to say that you don't trust me?' Roger's voice was icy.

'I hope there's no reason not to. After all, this is the first time personal feelings have come into it for you,' said Brenda nastily. The others knew that Roger did not have deep feelings for people, usually.

'Well, I've no personal feelings and, Roger, we'll sort her out well and truly if one syllable of this gets out.' George's voice was as hard as the others had ever heard it. 'And you can tell her, in no uncertain terms.'

Roger said nothing. The others fixed him with their gaze.

26

Finally it happened. As so often happens, Sorcha's tension eased
as the period of waiting dragged on and on. She had not forgotten
about the plan but had allowed it to slip towards the back of her
mind. Then on Monday, after she had come in from school, she
heard it on the five o'clock radio news. The Panrab Corporation
had received a warning that stocks of their baby food had been
contaminated. In the interests of public safety (ha, thought Sorcha, in the interest of keeping their good name and their profit)
they were withdrawing immediately all of their baby food products under their three different brand names. No reason had been
given for the alleged attack but Panrab would not give in to any
blackmail attempts. They had always traded honestly and openly
(including spraying their workers with DDT, sneered Sorcha
inwardly) and had the corporate aim of providing pure natural
products (what about the rain forests? said Sorcha). Measures
would be taken to ensure that this sort of tampering could not
happen again and all the withdrawn stocks would be destroyed
(oh my God, thought Sorcha, they'll be back in business in a
week. They'll probably be better off because people will have
sympathy for them). The Gardaí were following a definite line
of inquiry (has he left some trace? He probably has, for all his
talk and caution).

'What's the matter with you? You look pale,' Eoin asked. He
was home early from work and was getting Sorcha's dinner

ready. He and her mother were going to eat out that night, to Sorcha's relief. She wanted time to think about this.

'Oh, nothing,' she answered and went to leave the kitchen.

'Are you sure?' Eoin said, the concern obvious in his voice.

'Yes,' Sorcha almost snapped. 'Leave me alone.' She went to her room wondering how she was going to get through the evening without letting them know.

Downstairs, her mother had come in. 'You're not actually suggesting that she could be involved?'

'No, of course not. But you should have seen her when the news came on. She was lounging about the kitchen as usual and she just froze. She was totally shocked. I'm not sure I've ever seen anything like it.'

'Did you speak to her?'

'Yes and she didn't hear me at all. She just went pale.'

'Maybe she knows someone who's involved,' said Nuala.

'It's possible. Who knows what Roger and that crew are like? They could be any kind of weirdo. I'll tell you, this is serious. Think of it.'

'Yes. A baby could be killed. And for what? From what I heard they didn't even say. Maybe it was anarchists, which would rule her crowd out. They stand for something, after all. Anarchists, they're against everything, aren't they?'

Eoin said, 'They're against society and so on. Being part of it and all that.'

'That's the sort of thing she's been talking about lately, isn't it?' said Nuala.

'God, I hope she hasn't been stupid.' Eoin's voice was serious.

'I'll tell you, one way or the other, it's time we took all this nonsense in hand. We are her parents, after all.' Nuala was getting very anxious. 'I think I'll go and talk to her.'

'No. Leave her for now. We'll see her later.'

So Sorcha's parents went out and she had time to think undisturbed and recover her balance somewhat.

On Saturday morning Sorcha was on her own again in the house. She had heard nothing from Roger or any of the others. All she knew was what she heard on the news. Panrab claimed to have recovered all but a few jars of food and had warned everyone to destroy what they had bought or return it for a refund. The general reaction was outrage. Still no one seemed to know why the contamination had happened. Either they were pretending, to avoid bad publicity, or William had made a mess of the letter. Then on Wednesday a baby got sick and suddenly they (the unknown attackers) were blamed and called animals and savages. It turned out that the baby had a virus and the Panrab food it had been eating was untouched.

The doorbell rang and when Sorcha answered it Roger stepped inside. He wasted no time. 'Look, it's done. The cops are closing in. We've got to get out of here. Come on.' He left her no room to argue and just enough time to get her coat. 'Have you any money?' he asked. He spoke so definitely and urgently that Sorcha obeyed him without pause, getting what she had, a few pounds. He would not let her leave the house with him but went on ahead. A few minutes later she caught up with him at the bus stop.

'Where are we going?' Sorcha asked.

'Shut up. Talk about something else.' He was tense, worried. He looked about him while trying to seem as if he was not doing so. They got the bus to Rathfarnham and it was only when they were in Marley Park that he would speak openly.

'Look, Sorcha, they've been checking up on us. I don't know if William was stupid or what but they've called to George and Marian. They asked George about me. I've got to get away.'

'Roger don't worry. How could they suspect you?' said Sorcha, trying to comfort him.

'I don't know. You're the newest member of the group.' Even now he would not say the Circle. 'People wonder about your loyalty.'

'Who does? That's stupid. Do you? I bet it's George, that stuck-up ...'

'Sorcha, keep your voice down.'

'Why? There's no one here. It's October and it's freezing and everyone's at home.'

'Shut up. Now.' He was not asking but ordering. There was someone, a man with a dog, then and they said nothing until he had passed.

Roger took Sorcha's elbow in his arm. 'Sorcha, I've always liked you. It was my idea to get you in. Now, if you were not with us there'd be ...' He stopped. Sorcha did not like the tone of his voice. It sounded very menacing. She felt a shudder of fear. 'If I get caught it could be jail. That's how serious this is.'

'What are you going to do?' she asked.

'What we are going to do,' said Roger, putting emphasis on the "we", 'is get me out of the country. You are going to buy me a ticket from Dun Laoghaire to Holyhead. In the meantime I'm going to stay out of the way.' He emphasised the "I'm" this time.

Sorcha was quiet. She knew that this was putting her right in the front of things, in the firing line. If he was worried about her loyalty then having her in her own danger made sense. If she was going to be in trouble herself she would be less likely to give him away. She tried to convince him, as they walked, that she was fully behind him and had done nothing to betray him. He did not seem too convinced and the more she talked the less convincing she seemed to herself, so she gave up.

They left the park and walked up the road to Three Rock, past the house with the security gates and on to the upward winding path to the top, the one Sorcha knew so well. She wondered did Roger know this or was it just chance that brought him here.

About half way up the mountain he suddenly stopped and looked up and down. They had seen no one since leaving Marley and the path was empty. He took her hand, not as an affectionate gesture, but roughly, to take charge of her and said, 'In here.' They left the path and went among the trees. Through them they could see a patchy Dublin Bay and Dun Laoghaire harbour far below. A ferry was tied up at the pier. From that distance they could not tell if it was the Holyhead boat.

Out of sight of the path was a small makeshift shelter. It looked like a mound of branches and twigs carelessly thrown aside and it was not until Roger cleared the opening to it that Sorcha realised what it was. 'Here,' said Roger. They wriggled in. The spindly branches allowed a green light to fill the tiny space. There was a groundsheet and a single sleeping bag. At least, thought Sorcha, he's not expecting me to stay.

'This is where I'm staying until you get me organised,' he announced. He took out a wallet. 'Here's money. This won't be enough. You'll have to get the rest yourself.'

'How? How much will I need?'

'About twenty-five pounds.'

'I'll never be able to get that much.'

'You'll have to. You'd better manage it.'

'How?'

'That's up to you.' Roger's tone was even more menacing than before and Sorcha was anxious to go. He told her that he had enough food until Monday and that if she had not got everything ready by then she was to bring more.

After she left him Sorcha made her plans. She had fifteen pounds in the Post Office and she decided that the best way to get the rest without raising suspicions was to borrow it from one person. She would have to skip school on Monday to bring him food. It would be best to get the ticket on the same day, if she had the money by then. If she was caught mitching, it would be a problem explaining why. She could always make out that it showed how serious she was about being fed up with school.

When she got home it was well into the afternoon and very cold. The strength had already gone out of the light and evening was on the way. Even before she turned her key in the door it was pulled open by Eoin.

'What's going on? The Gardaí have been here.'

Sorcha could feel the muscles in her jaws slackening. She did not want her mouth to flop open like some kind of fish. She tried to look surprised without being shocked. The calm state which she had forced herself into ever since Roger had called was rapidly deserting her.

'Oh, what on earth did they want?' She tried to strike the right note with her voice.

'You! They wanted to talk to you!'

'To me? What for?' She could feel the note was false and made a huge effort to overcome it. 'Me? The Guards? What on earth could they want with me?' That sounded better to her. Roger had once told her that you got used to lying and when it was for a good cause it was the right thing to do. He had said that sometimes people hadn't the right to know and then it was perfectly all right not to tell them things and lying was often the only way of doing so. She remembered those words now and fought against the instinct to escape to her own room. If she could brave it out with her parents she would have a better chance with the Guards later. She was in no doubt that they would call back.

Eoin said, 'It's to do with that baby food business. Are you involved?' He looked pale, in shock. 'Your mother is in a panic. She's gone looking for you. We didn't even know where you were.'

Sorcha realised she should have left a note. 'I went walking. To Three Rock.' She remembered another thing Roger had said, to use as much truth as possible so that it would be harder to catch you out. Yet, she knew, even as she said it that it did not appear right. She would not usually head off like that without leaving a message, especially at that time of the year.

'What on earth for, without telling us?'

'Oh, I was just fed up, I suppose, and wanted to be on my own.' Sorcha was catching on fast. By saying this she was preparing the ground to explain away her mitching on Monday, if she got caught. Yet, despite this, now it would seem that it was connected with the Gardaí's visit. Silently she cursed them.

She didn't have long to wait and when they did call it was just like in films and yet not like that at all. There were two of them, big burly men. Their blue car with its giveaway radio aerial was parked outside. Sorcha had seen them arriving from her bedroom window and so had a few moments to prepare herself. She waited in her room until her mother called and then, her heart pounding, she went downstairs.

She went into the front room where the pair waited with her parents. 'Hi,' she said, as confidently as she could.

'Hello, Sorcha. I'm Detective Garda Tom Matthews. This is Detective Garda Roger O'Brien.' He was trying to be as pleasant as possible but Sorcha's already pounding heart leapt wildly out of control when she heard the second name. She felt dizzy and thought she would collapse and tried hard not to show it. Suddenly she thought that maybe it was not a coincidence and that they had pretended his name was Roger to see her reaction.

'We'd like to talk to Sorcha on her own, if we may, Mr and Mrs Rafferty,' said pleasant Detective Tom. Sorcha was waiting for Roger to be the nasty one of the pair.

Her parents were thrown into confusion for a few seconds and then both said, 'No, she's a minor. We'll stay.'

The detective was not pleased and they all heard a slight but obvious change in his voice. 'If you say so, we'll do it this way for now.' Sorcha flinched from the new threat in his tone.

'Sorcha,' Detective Tom went on, 'you've probably heard about the alleged contamination of Panrab baby food.' She noticed that he had said "alleged". Had Roger not actually done anything? She nodded. 'We're trying to find out who would have done such a thing. We know that you've been attending meetings of an environmental group.' She nodded again. 'We're calling on everyone involved in such like meetings.'

'What's the name of that group?' asked Roger suddenly.

Sorcha jumped. 'I don't know. I mean it doesn't have a name. We just have meetings. It's not a group really. Not as such.' She forced herself to stop. She felt that her voice was reasonably calm.

'As such?' asked Roger, exaggerated surprise in his voice. He stopped. The four of them looked at her, her parents drawn and anxious. No one said anything so she had to go on. 'Well, we have meetings. About things, the environment. It's not a group, really. Not as ...' She swallowed.

'Really?' Roger was even more surprised, almost incredulous, as he again repeated her words.

'I mean, there's no one in charge, as such.' There I go again, she moaned inside. 'We just have meetings. Lots of people come.'

'To the meetings?' His eyebrows rose. He did not smile. If they're trying to make me uncomfortable, they're succeeding, thought Sorcha.

'Did you ever discuss Panrab at these ... meetings?' asked Tom, still the more friendly.

'No.' She thought of Roger's advice about being truthful as far as possible. 'I mean yes.' She remembered Roger had said that they had been talking to some of the others and wondered had they denied it. 'That is, I think we did. We must have. We talked, talk that is, about everything connected with the environment.'

'Consciousness raising?' asked Roger, disbelievingly.

'What? Oh, yes,' answered Sorcha.

'How is Panrab connected to the environment?' asked Tom, sounding genuinely interested.

'Oh, you know, they exploit workers, use chemicals, destroy rain forests.' She was afraid of sounding too knowledgeable, so she said, 'You know, all the multi-nationals do.'

'So you're in favour of this contamination then,' said Roger, making it as much of a statement as a question.

'Yes. I mean no. Of course not.'

'Hold on,' said Nuala. 'Question her, but don't try to trip her up. She's only a kid.' Bless you, Mom, thought Sorcha.

The detective changed his course. 'Have you ever been involved in any illegal action in connection with this group?'

'No. Only legal ones. Like handing out leaflets.'

'Tell us about that,' said pleasant Tom.

Sorcha told them about the leaflets and about other activities organised by the Circle. She tried to mention names that were not part of it, people who would know nothing about them. It was after a long time, and it was just when she thought she was safe that Tom said, 'Tell us about Roger Darling.' Again she felt her heart race and her throat tighten. She thought she saw the two exchange glances, felt sure that they were suspicious. They were professionals, trained to notice people's reactions.

'Tell you what?' she asked. She didn't want to say anything unnecessary.

'Have you seen him this week? Since Monday?' The day of the contamination. They knew. She again remembered to tell as much truth as possible.

'I saw him this morning, for a few minutes. He called.' She thought she sounded the right casual note. Tom wrote in his notebook. The other Roger looked hard at her.

'What did he want?' he said.

'Oh, he just dropped in for a minute. To say he was going away. To visit his ... friends in the country.' She mentally kicked herself. They could check up on that. She remembered though, that he had told her that he had lived in the country. Perhaps he had friends there.

'Why did he need to tell you?' asked Roger. Sorcha noticed he said "need", as if he knew what was going on.

'He didn't need to. He told me because we're friends.'

'Is he your boyfriend?' asked Tom, a nasty edge in his voice, as if he thought anyone who had Roger for a boyfriend must be some dreadful, repulsive creature.

Nuala rescued her again. 'No, Guard. Sorcha has a boyfriend. A very nice boy, Paul. We know him well.' Tom asked for Paul's address and took it down.

'You're not going to question him, are you?' asked Sorcha. They must have heard the worry in her voice.

'Why?' asked Roger, nastily.

'Because he has nothing to do with ...'

'With what?' butted in Roger.

'With the group,' said Sorcha.

'So it's a group now,' he pounced.

'Yes. No. You know what I mean.'

'Do I? I think maybe I'm not sure. When will Darling be back?' He made Roger's name sound like a foul word.

'I don't know. He didn't say. Probably in a few days.' Sorcha stumbled over this. It was obvious that if he told her he was going he would tell her when he was coming back. Roger was right about the lies. They picked her up on it but she finally seemed to satisfy them. They asked more questions and mentioned George, the only other Circle member they talked about. She told them that she knew very little about him and only ever saw him at meetings, and then not often, which was basically true.

Finally they left, leaving her with the feeling that they were suspicious but said nothing about coming back. Sorcha knew that she would have to get Roger out quickly, before they called again, or began watching her.

Her parents, who knew that the interview had been difficult for her, didn't bother her afterwards. They hugged her and sat with her for a while. They too were suspicious and worried and Sorcha could see how hard it was for them. She was grateful for their understanding.

* * *

On Sunday morning she was walking on her own, near the shops on Drumcondra Road when she heard a voice behind her. 'Say nothing. If the cops call say nothing at all, I'm warning you.' It was George. He was walking faster than she was and was nearly past her as he finished speaking. He did not look at her, pretending to be a stranger.

'Roger's gone,' she said. He was forced to slow down and walk beside her.

'Were you involved?' His voice was low, half hiss, half whisper, all vicious undertone.

'Yes. I went with him.' They did not look at each other, keeping up the pretence of being strangers.

'How long is he staying there?' George obviously knew of the hide-out.

'Until tomorrow, or Tuesday. The cops have been to see me.'

'What did you tell them?' he almost snarled.

'Nothing. They were looking for Roger.' They still did not look at each other.

'Damn. What did you tell them?'

'Nothing. I already told you.'

'Well, keep it that way, do you hear, for your own sake.' With that parting shot he accelerated and was gone.

27

Every news report on Sunday was full of it. A jar of poisoned baby food had been found in a southside city supermarket. There were interviews with Garda chiefs, with politicians, with priests, with community leaders, with spokespeople for the mainstream environmental groups, with supermarket executives, with Panrab chiefs, with parents, with the ISPCC, with young people, with, it seemed to Sorcha, everyone in the country. They all said the same thing, that this attack was an outrage and no cause whatsoever could possibly justify it. Sorcha felt extremely nervous at the thought of so many people being against her, and yet she knew that they had done this for only the very best of reasons. For the first time since they had decided on the action she had a rush of doubt about the whole business. It was very hard to hold on to her belief when it seemed that literally everyone despised it. They, of course, did not understand why it was being done, for what good reasons. The worst moment of all was when the lunch-time television news showed a picture of a jar like the contaminated one and she saw the picture of the smiling, happy baby filling the screen. Even though she knew that Panrab used these pictures and hid the awful things they did she quite literally shuddered at the thought of a little baby eating some horrible poisoned food.

Her parents were watching the news with her and Eoin switched off the set as soon as that item ended. They explained their worry to her, saying that they trusted her but that there must be some reason for the Gardaí calling. She told them that they were calling to everyone involved in groups like hers, that it was routine. They asked her whether she would tell him if there was anything going on. At that moment, they seemed so trusting and supportive that she almost let go and told them everything. Then she remembered Roger in his shelter, his money in her pocket, George on the street, and held back. She assured them that she would. Finally they seemed satisfied. Sorcha felt guilty but comforted herself with the thought that sometimes, for the greater good, the full truth simply had to be hidden. The old world that she was fighting was riddled with deceit and dishonesty and fire had to be fought with fire.

She was on her own then and went for a walk. All the feelings and the worry were getting too much and she decided that she would have to talk to someone, to get some advice, or at least just to get it off her chest for a while. She thought of Conor. He was always very understanding and even though he would disapprove he would listen, and not condemn her. The problem was that he was off with Sally, his girlfriend and would not be back until late. As well as that there was the problem that they were not really as close as they had been. Ever since the row in the summer when she had attacked him, he was quite distant. Even if he had been around she was not altogether sure that she could tell him everything.

She turned a corner and the wind blew, cold and damp, lifting her coat and hair. She dug her hands deeper into her pockets and looked towards the mountains away across the city. Behind Three Rock, thick black clouds were gathering. The sky above her was still bright but over there it looked like night, even though it was early afternoon. The thought of Roger huddling, scared for all his brave talk, frozen and alone filled her thoughts, blackening them as the clouds blackened the sky. The weak sun did nothing to warm her. In a few minutes the darkness would have reached it and the cold would be worse, the day more gloomy. She wanted to help Roger because she felt like this, sorry for him and scared for him, as well as because she was afraid of him and afraid of George.

She thought of Paul. She could talk to him. He would be glad that she needed him, glad that she was confiding in him. He always seemed to think she was too independent. She could imagine him holding her in his arms. The thought of that nearly pushed away the effect of the wind and looming clouds. He would be able to tell her what to do and make her feel good. She was turning in the direction of his house when she imagined what he would say when she told him. He would be shocked and angry, confused, even hurt. He would think that she was crazy and would not be able to understand at all why they did it. The wind blew so cold and hard it pained her ears. She knew she couldn't go to Paul.

Brenda had always been nice to her, had been pleased when she joined the Circle. She could try talking to her. It was quite a distance to her flat. She decided to take the bus, thinking all the time of Roger and how he hated doing anything that was part of the polluting process, how she had walked to Brenda's before, with him. The thought that his safety depended on her, and on her alone, make her feel sick. She hoped that Brenda would be in.

Sorcha knew she shouldn't call. They had agreed that there would be no contact between them until it was all over. As she stood at the door she ran through her explanation, her excuse in fact, again. She rang the bell and strained her ears to listen for sounds inside. Finally an inner door opened and she thought she heard a voice. Then there were footsteps and the metallic undoing of the lock. Sorcha was not breathing and her heart pounded.

'Hello,' she said, 'I just ...'

Brenda's mouth flopped. She looked quickly up and down the street. 'You,' she hissed. 'Were you seen?'

Sorcha was not prepared for this. Brenda reached out, grabbed her wrist and yanked her inside. 'No. I checked. It's OK, Brenda.'

'What do you mean it's OK? It's not OK. What are you doing here? Are you a complete fool?' Her voice was at normal volume and full of anger.

'I just wanted to talk to you, that's all,' said Sorcha, more miserable and regretting that she had come.

'About what? I don't want the cops here.' A cat had come out through a slightly ajar door off the hall and was rubbing itself around Brenda's legs. It looked at Sorcha with its green indifferent eyes and she could hear its engine-like purr.

'Look, Brenda, I'm sorry I came. I'm worried and there was no-one else to talk to.'

'Why do you need someone to talk to? You're supposed to be self reliant. You don't need shoulders to cry on, you know.'

Sorcha was struck by the coldness in her attitude. She had never been like that before, or if she had Sorcha had not noticed it. She would have liked, even then, to go into one of the rooms and sit down with Brenda and talk to her but she was not invited. She felt uncomfortable and unwelcome in the hall. A second cat, a black one, slipped out through the door and rubbed its head against Brenda's ankle. Sorcha wanted to see what was in the room. More cats? Brenda was very keen on animals. A boy? She was keen on boys as well. If there was anyone there they would be able to hear anything said in the hall.

'It's Roger really. I'm scared for him. He called yester ...'

'That's your end of it, Sorcha,' Brenda broke in instantly. 'You're there to help with problems. If there's a problem, the less I know the better, for all of us.' She bent and scooped up the black cat and began stroking its head. It narrowed its eyes with pleasure. She waited for Sorcha to speak.

Sorcha knew that she was right. She was weak to need to talk. The thought that she had nearly gone to Paul or Conor terrified her. She suddenly felt unworthy of the Circle. She wondered how they could have let her in when she was so unsuitable. 'Sorry, Brenda. I've been stupid. I'll go now,' she said.

'You haven't spoken to anyone else? Anyone outside, I mean,' asked Brenda, staring hard at Sorcha.

'Do you think I can't be trusted either?' Sorcha almost wailed. She glanced at the open door again and held back, did not tell Brenda about the Gardaí. 'Of course I didn't.' She had the distinct feeling that there was someone in the room.

'You'd better be trustworthy. You'd better. If Roger needs you, don't fail him. That will not be tolerated. I'll see to it, Sorcha. Nothing had better go wrong.' The cat, at her voice jumped from her arms and fled back to the room, through the door. The other one was sitting under a table, still looking at her.

Brenda opened the door, looked up and down the street and said, 'Go now.' She pushed Sorcha out.

Brenda went back into the sitting room. The black cat was on the couch beside George. 'I think she got the message,' said Brenda.

'You did well,' said George, 'come here.'

Brenda scooped the cat off the couch and sat under his protective arm. 'We'll be all right, you'll see,' he said as he bent to kiss her.

28

Sorcha stayed awake late that night, making her plans. Roger had told her to be back with food on Monday. It was not going to be possible to get the money and the ticket in time for then. She knew that it would be too risky to skip school on two days so she decided that he would have to wait until Tuesday. She hoped he wouldn't be too hungry. The thought of his having no food filled Sorcha with unease. She imagined that she would not survive without one meal, never mind a whole day's.

Sorcha's plan complete, she tried to sleep but started awake each time she was almost gone, then sat up, turned on the light, checked the time, found it was ten minutes since the last time, tried to stop grinding her teeth, went to the toilet, fixed the sheets where her tossing had crumpled them, until the final start was too weak to disturb her and her breathing came evenly, her heart slowed and her limbs rested.

As she finally sank to sleep Roger left his cramped uncomfortable shelter. The rain which had threatened since morning had held off and the sky had partly cleared. That, unfortunately for him, was the only good that there was about his situation. He was cold, colder than he had ever been, even though he was wrapped in a parka jacket, a woollen cap covered his ears, a scarf his face and heavy gloves his hands. Still his fingers were numb, his ears ached and his feet in his climbing boots and woollen socks were no more than blocks of ice. His joints and muscles were stiff and sore. He had handled his rations badly and had emptied his flask by lunch hour. All he had left was a lump of goat's cheese, which was not terribly fresh.

He had slept most of the day and his face was scratched from the branches and twigs in his shelter. Very few people had passed. They were real walkers, most of them, beginning the Wicklow Way or another long walk. Only one of the couples he saw passing returned. They had lasted only half an hour in the cold. Then he had glimpsed them from his shelter, huddled together for warmth and comfort, wearing only jeans and runners and light jackets, as they hurried back to their parked car.

Now at least, he could walk the path towards the top of the mountain. There was unlikely to be anyone about. The stars were like brilliant dust strewn from the clouds into the gaps between them. Here there was little pollution and they shone beautifully. He had heard, on his walkman, that one of his jars had been found. If the stars were to be seen like this, by future generations, then actions like his were necessary. And this would be worth it. He became so lost in his thoughts that he was startled when he turned a bend and saw the red warning lights on the transmitters. He walked over to them and stood by one of the rocks. Below the city twinkled its way around the curve of the bay. Howth, Dun Laoghaire, houses, people, all being destroyed by factories, cars. He looked again at the sky and the sparkling of the stars. They seemed so pure to him, so full of mystery, so awe-inspiring. As he looked, the glowing ember of a shooting star streaked across the black sky, slowly extinguishing as it passed the line of the bay. He remembered a line that a teacher had read to him at school: 'The eternal silence of these infinite spaces terrifies me.' The natural world was terrifying to Roger in its hugeness and wonder but also in its delicate balance that humans could so easily destroy, in its beauty that could be ruined. He respected nature as it was. He saw no reason to interfere with it and was glad again that he was doing something to protect the 'infinite spaces'. He turned to go down the mountain, to his shelter. He hoped Sorcha would come early with food.

The clouds were thickening again and the dim light from the sky faded. He stumbled his way back, eventually having to use his torch, carefully shading it so that the light was directed downwards.

He did not remember other lines read to him by the same teacher:

They cannot scare me with their empty spaces
Between stars — on where no human race is.
I have it in me so much nearer home
To scare myself with my own desert places.

* * *

Sorcha had decided to ask Pam for the fifteen pounds she needed. The only reason she didn't take it from her parents was that she was afraid they might notice it missing and there was so much suspicion around the house that they would automatically think of her. That thought troubled her because before it would never have occurred to them that she might take money from them, nor would it have occurred to her to take it.

There was not much else that she could do that day except wait. She got herself out to school and through the first three classes automatically. She was vaguely surprised to find the right books in her bag because she did not remember putting them there. The only thing she was really aware of was listening to the eight o'clock news. It was the third item and no new jars had been discovered. Garda investigations were 'continuing' and still following a 'definite line of inquiry'. She thought of the two detectives and of Roger, waiting for her and his supplies. Roger must be the definite line of inquiry. She hoped that they wouldn't come back to her again. She didn't think she could handle it. She imagined breaking down and telling them everything and it seemed as if that would be the easiest thing to do. Then she would explain why she had done it, everyone would understand and she could be normal again. The worry, the fear of being caught, the fighting would disappear. But she knew, even as she thought of it, that she could not do that. She had got involved of her own free will and now Roger needed her. Then there was George and, it seemed, Brenda as well. Who knows what they would do to her if Roger was caught?

At the eleven o'clock break, before Sorcha had time to ask Pam for the money, she said, 'Hey, Sorcha, what's up with you? You look as if you've been up in the mountains all night.'

'What do you mean by that?' snapped Sorcha.

'Sorry for living. Nothing. You look like something the cat brought in, that's all.'

Brenda flashed into Sorcha's mind, coldly cat-stroking. She realised she would have to control what she said or she would give herself away. And if she wanted to get money from Pam she had better be nice to her. 'Pam, listen, have you any money? I need to borrow some.'

Pam was surprised. 'Sure, Sorcha. Hey, is anything the matter? I mean, are you all right?'

'Yes. I just need fifteen quid. I'm being blackmailed by a Middle Eastern heroin smuggler who has discovered that I once copied my History homework from you and is now threatening to tell Porky unless I cough up the fifteen punts.' Sorcha had to make a big effort to be light-hearted.

Pam laughed. 'Remember that! That was in second year and you were bawling because you hadn't done it. Some cousin you'd fancied had called, if I remember.'

'Yeh. I stayed up and decided, to hell with the ecker. Then, next morning I was in a state. Boy, did I regret my careless abandon then. But you saved my skin, Pam. Save it now, will you, and give me the fifteen quid, if you have it?'

'I have it, in the Post Office. I'll get it tomorrow.'

'No. Now. Today, I mean. This evening, after school.' Sorcha forced herself to stay cool. 'Ram-al-Rashad will be after me tonight.'

'Oh, OK. This evening then. I'll bring ... '

'No. I'll come home with you and get it. If that's all right with you.'

'Sure, Sorcha, that's OK.' Pam sounded most unsure.

Later on, as Sorcha went home with Pam while she got her savings book and then went to the Post Office while she got the money, it was difficult to keep up normal conversation. Sorcha knew that Pam was dying to ask what it was really for and she was determined to talk of anything except that. They even got round to the contamination and she could not cut Pam short, for fear of making her suspicious.

'They're real swine, those people. Imagine a little baby being poisoned,' said Pam.

'Yeh, but none were,' said Sorcha, not wanting to have to act too much, so staying with the 'being as truthful as possible' principle.

'That's not the point. They tried.'

'How do you know? They gave a warning. Maybe they just wanted publicity for their cause.'

'What cause?' said Pam, derisively.

'Oh, I don't know. That Panrab is a big multi-national. They do a lot of damage to the planet.'

'So, your crowd would support it, I suppose,' said Pam, it never actually occurring to her that people she knew, or even knew of, could be involved in such a thing.

'Yes, in a way. I suppose they would,' said Sorcha.

'That's disgusting. Do you? Do you agree with poisoning babies?' said Pam angrily.

'No, I don't agree with poisoning babies. But Panrab poisons its workers, and the rain forests and they do it deliberately, to make cutesy baby foods for the West. I support trying to stop them and if ...' Here Sorcha stopped.

'What were you going to say? If that means poisoning babies you'd go along with it?' Sorcha said nothing, so Pam went on. 'If it was your own brother or cousin or your own baby that's not how you'd feel.'

Finally Sorcha got the money and went home, feeling more confused than ever. The evening news had moved the story down to near the end of the bulletin. No new information had come in and the Gardaí reported no new developments. Sorcha went to her room to study but didn't even try when she got there. She spent most of the evening looking out her window and more than once nearly crying out when a dark coloured car drove near. She half-expected the guards to come back to her.

* * *

Tuesday morning was bright and dry and Sorcha was thankful for that. She had to get dressed and ready for school as usual. Her father was always the last to leave so she would have to go out and come back after he had gone. During the news her parents began discussing a report of an explosion in Belfast and Sorcha barely heard the newsreader say that Gardaí wanted to interview Roger Darling in connection with the Panrab contamination. She nearly choked on her muesli and immediately enthusiastically joined in her parents' discussion in order to keep them distracted.

* * *

Away up in his hideaway Roger was colder than ever. He had waited all through Monday. By eleven he was worried and by one he nearly panicked. He was faint with hunger and sure Sorcha had deserted him. As the afternoon dragged on he thought of leaving but had nowhere to go. Sorcha had most of his money and he was afraid to risk going home. He really had no choice but to wait. His impatience and anger at her grew as the light left the day. The night had been terrible. Every sound had been the Gardaí, every movement filled him with terror. His sleep had been fitful and short. He was stiff and sore. He got up at first light on Tuesday, deciding to give her until eleven. Then he would have to risk going, no matter what. If she had squealed on him he would kill her. The others were right, she shouldn't have been trusted. Yet along with these thoughts ran the hope that something had happened, that she couldn't come yesterday, that she would come now. When he heard on the news that they were looking for him he knew that he'd have to go, somehow. He would call to George for help, no matter what the danger.

Sorcha gave her father ten minutes to be clear and then came back. She hoped none of the neighbours noticed. Anything unusual might be remembered later, if someone decided to jog their memories. Before she opened the hall door a quick look up and down the road showed no one. Inside she went straight to the kitchen and put some bread, salad, a pint of milk, fruit and nuts into a shopping bag. 'That'll have to do him,' she said as she finished and went back to the hall. She already had the money and her savings book in her school bag. She would have to bring the school bag with her in case her mother came in before her and found it there. She sometimes came home early, if she had a meeting later on.

She was moving quietly in the empty, silent house. The voice came out of nowhere. 'What are you doing here?' Sorcha's heart failed, her breath deserted her after having being expelled in an animal-like grunt which she heard as if it came from outside her. Lightness splashed over her head, making the hallway spin. She almost dropped the bag of provisions and had to grasp the kitchen door handle for support.

'Dad! What are ... ? Why ...? I thought you were at work. Wow, you scared me.'

'Hey, I can see that. Are you OK?' He put his arm around her shoulders, smiling. 'I should have thought and called out. I didn't know who it was. Got a bit of a fright myself. Are you OK?'

'Yes. I'm fine now,' Sorcha said, her heart still pounding, her legs shaking.

'What are you doing here anyhow? Mitching I suppose,' joked Eoin.

Sorcha tried to smile but it felt like a grimace to her. 'That's right, Dad. I'm skipping off school today.'

'Ah, no, what are you doing, really?'

By this time Sorcha's brain was starting to work again. 'There's a sale of work in aid of famine relief and I forgot all about it. I came back to get some stuff.' She held up the bag. He had not noticed it up to then and seemed satisfied with her explanation. It occurred to Sorcha that she should have said nothing about it but then she changed her mind. He might have remembered, later on, if he was called on to.

'Well, do you need a note for being late?'

'No. I'm OK I'll go on. I'll be in time, just. Bye.' She went to the door. 'Hey, why aren't you at work? Mitching?'

'I told you at breakfast. I've got a meeting. It's not till half nine.'

'Sorry. I forgot.' She went out, cursing herself for being so stupid. She hadn't listened and if she had she would have left him more time to get out and away. The Post Office was near his bus stop into town. She couldn't afford the risk of his seeing her there. She couldn't go near school either, in case someone spotted her. The day was beautiful but cold, and she didn't want to hang about but she had no choice. She walked for a few minutes but there were too many girls from her school and she was afraid that they would notice her. It was unfortunate that she had to wear her uniform, as it made her so conspicuous. On the other hand she blended in with all the school-going uniforms. She decided to walk towards school in the hope that she would not be noticed in the flow.

The girl ahead was in her class and they often walked together. Sorcha had to slow down so that she would not catch up with her. Once or twice the girl half-turned and Sorcha jumped. If she saw her it would be impossible to escape. No matter how slowly she went she gained on the girl. Sorcha stopped and opened and re-tied her shoelace. She had to walk on and in a few moments was almost up with her again. The girl waved at another crossing the road. The second girl was sure to see Sorcha who was just then passing a lane so she turned into it. Here were garages and rear garden walls. As long as no one came out in their car she would be safe, at least for a short time. She could think of no good explanation for her being there, if someone did arrive. The lane was no short cut, just a dead end. There was some rubbish against a wall, a few empty beer cans and the trace of a fire. Someone had had a party there recently. It was the sort of lane the Gardaí patrolled, although most likely at night.

After a few minutes she decided it was safer back in the street. The school uniforms were gone. It was just after nine. The girls, except for the inevitable few stragglers, would be in school. She headed back the way she had come, walking slowly to give her father time to be well clear. She felt as if everyone was staring at her. Some mothers were coming out now to do their shopping. She was sure they they would wonder why she was out of school, walking in the wrong direction, and in uniform. She hoped none of them would recognise her. When she reached the main road she had a bad moment while she checked the people at the bus stop. Her father was not there. Of course, she thought, he could be late and not have arrived yet. She would have to take that risk.

So it was with sweaty palms and shortness of breath that she went into the Post Office and got her money with, to her temporary relief, no problem. There was a travel agent beside the Post Office and she had to fight hard to control her voice, to sound calm, when she got there. She must have looked strange in her school uniform buying a one-way ticket to Holyhead. If she'd had the money she would have got the ticket the day before and saved all of this. She imagined that the assistant, a good looking fellow only a few years older than herself, must have been able to see her stomach churning.

He leaned on the counter, not hurrying. 'So, you're eloping, are you?' he asked.

Sorcha thought of Simone and of how she would handle this. She smiled and tossed her hair. Looking him straight in the eyes she leaned slightly towards him and said, in as husky a voice as she could manage, 'No, actually, it's for my brother. I'll be around for a while yet. I'm going to see him off.' 'Lucky brother,' he said. 'Thank you,' said Sorcha thinking, Boy, you're some creep. She waited for the ticket. He seemed to go slowly, deliberately, to hold her there. It occurred to her that playing Simone was not that difficult. Finally she was out on the street. There was still no sign of her father so she decided that he was gone and that she was safe, at least for the moment.

She got the bus to Rathfarnham and began the long walk to Three Rock. She hoped that if anyone saw her that they would know her uniform was not local, assume that she was mitching and smile indulgently, remembering their own school days.

29

By the time she had reached the place where she had left Roger, Sorcha was sweating and short of breath. She had never walked the path so quickly, almost at a run. When Roger showed her his hide-out she had marked a huge tree in her mind as a signpost to help her find the place again. The tree in front of her looked like the one but she could not see any sign of the shelter among the undergrowth at the side of the path, where it should be. She remembered that Dublin Bay could be glimpsed through the trees at the spot but that was not really much help now as it could be seen from quite a number of places. She had not noticed the shelter on Saturday until she was almost on top of it and wondered should she leave the path now in the hope of finding it. She looked at her watch. It was a quarter past eleven. If she wasted time trying to find him he would miss the ferry, due to leave at three o'clock. She looked up and down the path. It was empty. She thought of calling out. Surely, though, he would be looking out for her and would see her if she passed. She looked at her watch again. She looked at the tree. That was it, she was in no doubt.

Deciding, she turned to her left and jumped down off the raised track and plunged in among the trees. She tore at one pile of twigs, then another. Nothing. The sea sparkled at her through the branches. She could just see the end of the pier at Dun Laoghaire, where the ferry would soon dock. Her breathing was more difficult now and she was panting. She turned left and downwards but the way was blocked by impenetrable tangle and undergrowth. Right and upwards was clearer but there was still no sign as she pulled herself along. 'Roger,' she pleaded aloud, half moan, half whisper. She clambered back to the path, catching her skirt and tearing a seam. She couldn't see her school bag, or the bag of food which she had left at the edge of the path. Her first thought was that someone had taken them but she dismissed it because she was sure there was no one about. As she looked down, trying to locate the exact spot at which she had dropped them and gone searching, a movement across at the far side of the path caught her attention. There was no bright glare of light in among the trees there because the mountain sloped upwards behind them, blocking out the skyline and making that part of the forest much darker. She stayed as still as possible, with her pounding heart and rasping breath. Drops of sweat ran from her forehead into her eyes and she impatiently wiped them off with her sleeve. Everything was still and now that she was still herself, and listening, she became conscious of the birds singing, echoing all around her. There was no movement and after an interminable age she moved herself, taking a few steps across the narrow path. There was a flutter, a brush of branch and grass and the raised, reddish brown fur of a fox's tail retreating made her laugh aloud with relief. She turned and saw the bags, in a slight hollow and clearly visible from this vantage point.

She walked on, the path snaking to the right and then to the left again, the downward slope and the sea once more on her left. There, now was her big tree, no mistake this time, she was sure. Gingerly she approached and waited and then, in an urgent whisper, 'Sorcha? Get off the path!' She was so relieved she leapt down at him, dropped her bags and threw her arms around him. 'Oh, Roger, I'm sorry. I've been so worried.'

He pulled her arms away roughly. 'Where the hell have you been? It's Tuesday, for crying out loud. Are you alone? Does anyone know you're here? Are you sure?' Sorcha had answered his second two questions, leaving aside for the moment the longer explanation demanded by the first. She was taken aback by his obvious anger. 'Yes, I'm sure,' she said to his last one.

'You bloody well left me up here all this time in the freezing cold with no food. There'd better be a good reason. I've sacrificed everything for the Circle. What have you done? Sat on your backside by the fire and done your stupid homework.' Roger was inspired by Sorcha's uniform. 'I was just about to leave. I hope you got the ticket.'

There was so much menace in his voice that she was very glad to be able to say, 'Yes, Roger, I have it here. For the three o'clock sailing.' That seemed to pacify him a little. 'I had to wear the uniform so they'd think I was going to school. Look, I've brought food.' Each of these statements helped as well, so that by the time Roger began eating he was almost friendly, but not so friendly that she would think of touching him again. Sorcha looked at her watch and was amazed to find that it was twenty past eleven, only five minutes since she had begun looking for the shelter.

By half past they were well on their way back down the mountain. Roger had eaten and was insisting on going home before going to the ferry. Sorcha had advised him against it: they didn't have enough time, and she felt he was putting himself at unnecessary risk. He had left in such a hurry that he had not brought enough clothes and he said that there were a few things at home he wanted to have with him and that he had no intention of leaving unprepared. He said that the case was not important enough for the Gardaí to be watching his house.

As the bus rocked and rattled its way across the city Sorcha's uneasiness increased. She could sense an attitude in Roger that she had not known before. He was cold and withdrawn and uncaring. He was wound up like a spring, all jittery and unpredictable. She felt that he could turn on her at any time. He hadn't once asked her how she was and didn't seem to care. For these reasons, when she had explained the delay in getting to him she left out the visit by the Gardaí completely. She felt safer not mentioning it even if that was being disloyal to the openness the members of the Circle demanded of each other. She was increasingly sure that the Circle, or at least part of it, was not open with her.

It was just after one when they arrived in Drumcondra. They were both aware of the danger of being caught so close to home. Sorcha was annoyed, increasingly, as they got near his house, that he was prepared to expose her to this extra risk. It was his business if he wanted to put himself in danger but it wasn't fair to do it to her. She said nothing about it and neither did Roger, as if the idea had not even occurred to him. She did think about not going to the ferry with him but she knew he was expecting her to be there and did not know how to refuse him.

'Why don't they devote their time to stopping the horrors of companies like Panrab instead of chasing people like me, who are trying to save them all?' he said angrily as they walked. He kept the hood of his jacket up but Sorcha felt very exposed in her uniform coat. There were a few girls from her school going back after lunch but these were on bicycles and at this distance from school had to rush to get home and back and would be unlikely to notice her. She kept close to Roger, away from the road, for protection, like ladies in the old days did, she compared quietly to herself. She did not feel like talking to him.

They were leaving his house which, to Sorcha's relief had been empty, before half past one. He threw a coat at her and said, 'Wear this.' She was glad as it gave her some protection, by hiding her uniform. Roger checked at the front window before opening the hall door. 'It's the cops,' he said. She ran to his side. A patrol car was easing its way along the road. It stopped outside the house and the two Gardaí peered out. One got out of the car, cap in hand, and looked up and down the road. Roger put his finger to his lips, to warn Sorcha to be quiet. She glared at him. Did he think she was stupid? She took his arm and pulled him away from the window, into the dark of the room. They could see the Garda coming up the garden, adjusting his cap on his head, before the window frame hid him from view.

After a few moments the door-bell rang. There was a pause, every muscle they possessed tensed to breaking point, ears paining from the strain of listening. The bell rang again and they both jumped, involuntarily. Even now Sorcha did not want to clutch at Roger. If it had been almost anyone else standing there she would have. The Garda's radio cackled and was silent. He banged the knocker loudly. They stared at the bright rectangle of window and could see the blue car outside. The Garda still in it was reading a newspaper. Almost before the sound of the knocker had faded the figure of the first Garda, large and peering, appeared at the window. His hands were to his eyes, to provide shade while he looked in. Sorcha and Roger, as one, stepped silently backwards into the hall. Neither breathed until his shape darkened the bubbled glass of the hall door again. He hammered the knocker, its surprisingly high pitched sound reverberating in the house. Before one knock had faded the next followed, building up to a window-rattling cacophony. Then the fragmented figure shrank and faded away from the doorlight.

Breaths coming in short gasps they carefully put their heads around the sitting room door in time to see the car pull away, two Gardaí inside. 'Let's get the hell out of here,' said Sorcha. She pulled her disguising coat tightly around her and went to the door.

Sorcha had a worrying feeling that there had been a third Garda who was waiting for them to come out. She wanted Roger to go on ahead and she would follow, as they had done from her house a few days earlier. He would not agree. 'You're in this now with me, up to the hilt.' They left together, as quickly a possible and tried to look casual once the house was behind them. At least Sorcha felt less uncomfortable with her uniform hidden. By two o'clock they were sitting on the bus for Dun Laoghaire, the journey into town having been quick and uneventful. 'We should make it, if we're lucky,' said Sorcha. Roger said nothing.

Ever since the day before, a thought had been niggling at Sorcha. Pam had asked her would she support poisoning a baby for the cause. She had never really believed that it would go that far, that it might happen. After talking to Pam she thought of all the people who could have bought one of the bottles. She thought of herself, if she had a baby of her own and how she would feel if it was poisoned. There was a real risk that someone could have unknowingly killed their own child. The thought made her shiver. She would be responsible, as well as Roger and the others. The certain knowledge that it could not be right weighed heavily on her. The bus hit a pothole and every part of her jarred. The driver seemed intent on setting a new speed record for the journey and it was an old bus whose suspension had seen better days. Sorcha found it hard to think clearly. She looked at Roger beside her. His hands were clamped on the bar of the seat in front. She could see the whitish patches where his tightly bent fingers were made bloodless. His head darted from side to side, now looking out the window, now at the driver, now at the other passengers. He seemed totally unaware of her. Every now and then he said, 'Come on, you fool, come on.' The constant rattling got momentarily worse as the bus passed over a stretch of recently excavated ground. Her head rattled, her brain rattled. Suddenly she wanted to test Roger, to see what he really stood for.

'Roger,' she said.

'Yes,' he said, abruptly.

'About that baby,' she hesitated.

He looked at her for the first time since they got on the bus. 'What baby?' he asked.

She indicated the earphones of his walkman, hooped idly about his neck. 'Have you not been listening to the news?'

'Not since eight. I was too tense waiting for you.' He waited.

'A baby was poisoned. Somewhere like Rathmines, or Rathgar. Maybe Rathfarnham. The southside anyway. This morning. It's in intensive care.'

'Oh, God. Why didn't you tell me?' The last few words came out in the half-full, rattling bus as a choking whisper. Sorcha began to feel she had misjudged him. He said, 'That was why they were at the house. This is serious now. Will it die?'

'They seem to think it will. They got it too late. The mother ... ,' Sorcha paused, looking sad and upset, 'didn't realise what was wrong or they could have pumped its stomach.'

'Stupid, stupid, stupid,' he almost wailed.

'It's OK, Rog. We were all stupid. How could we not have seen this might ...'

'I mean the woman. The stupid mother. Did she not listen to the news? We're in really big trouble now.'

'But, Roger. What about ...? Don't you care about ...? I mean the baby, its parents. What about that?' Sorcha could hardly put words on what she was thinking. She shook and rattled as the bus charged on.

'Tough about them, sure. It's a risk we all took. Had to take. Look, Sorcha, it wasn't suppose to happen. You know that. They'll never believe it, though. Blast the stupid woman.'

'Roger, you don't care about the baby, at all.' Sorcha finally shaped her thought.

'We haven't time to care too much about small situations, small lives. We're changing the world. Making it better. That's what counts. Blast her. Blast, blast, blast.'

Sorcha said nothing more after that. The bus landed just after twenty to three and they ran to the ferry. They arrived pantingly and looked for signs of watchful Gardaí before Roger checked through. As he was going he said, 'We made it. Sorcha, keep up the work. Keep up the Circle.' He turned and was gone. He hadn't said one personal word, one word of friendship or of sorrow. She didn't tell him that there was no baby, that she had made it up, to test him.

It was ten to three when she last saw him, boarding the boat. By nine minutes to three she was in a phone box making a call. She went to a place on the pier where she could watch the boat and found a seat. Inside, she was numb. Her mind, as if hammered by the bus journey and all that had happened in the last weeks, months even, was blank. She just sat and watched and waited.

Three o'clock. The boat did not move. She had often watched the crew casting off, often wishing that she was with the crowds on deck watching the harbour slip silently behind, the people shrinking, new places opening up in front. Now the crew made no moves, just lounged there, chatting. The car deck had been closed, the gangplanks withdrawn. No one could board the boat - or leave it.

Ten past three. Sorcha still sat, her body now numbing from the cold. Others who waited moved about. She could hear, as if from a great distance, people wondering what was the delay. On deck passengers were asking the crew, some of whom talked into radios and raised their hands in helplessness. She could not see Roger.

At twenty past three, three Garda squad cars and two un-marked cars swept in convoy into the embarkation area, blue lights flashing. At least ten Gardaí, uniformed and plain clothes emerged and went to the ship. A gangway was put in place and taken away when they had boarded. There was a buzz of excited chatter among the people around Sorcha. On the upper deck more than one person looked nervously at the rushing officers. Sorcha still sat, watching. Some of the Gardaí were armed and the sight of the short barreled, makeshift-looking machine guns filled her with terror. It was the first thing she had felt since making her phone call.

She sat there until four o'clock. By then the light was weaken-ing, the day all but finished. Behind her, the sky was pink and grey, streaked with dappled cloud. Sorcha's breath clouded about her head. She could no longer feel her hands or feet but was beginning to wake from her reverie. Her terror, which had subsided, was replaced by anxiety. She began to worry about the consequences of what she had done, about Roger, about George and Brenda, about her parents and Paul, about, most of all, the Gardaí.

Just after four, a gangplank went up and there was a flurry of activity on the boat, the deck now dusky, except for the pools of brightness under the lamps. The troop of Gardaí moved down and she could clearly see Roger's face, lit briefly from above as he passed the swinging light at the top of the steep steps. Then he was in the gloomy shadows of the embarkation building and she could only make out his figure.

She stood up and began to stamp her feet to get her circulation going and watched until Roger was put in a car and the convoy blared and flashed its way out of the harbour.

Sorcha didn't know what she was going to do. She walked rapidly away towards the town, warming again from the movement. She heard the hooter of the ferry as it pulled away and was sure that she had done the right thing. She did not know what would happen to her as a result. Roger would be unlikely to name any of the others, or to give her away, because if she was arrested there was the danger that she might name them all. She went to a café in the main street and drank a cup of tea and ate a scone. Feeling warm and refreshed she went to a phone box.

'George, Sorcha here.' She waited for his reaction.

There was a pause and she wouldn't have been surprised if he had hung up. Then he said, 'What do you want?'

'It's over, George. Roger was arrested on the ferry. I'm quitting. I'm out of the Circle.'

'What do you mean you're out?' After his initial hesitation George was cool and in control again. 'It's not that easy, Sorcha.'

'George, it is that easy. I'm out.'

'You know too many things. I warned you. If you're responsible for Roger's ...'

'I'm out. I know nothing, George. And I know everything. If anything happens to me it'll all be told. I've made arrangements. Remember that.' Sorcha hung up. She wished she felt as confident as she had tried to sound.

She walked back towards the city. She could wait for a bus along the way when she got tired. She hoped her parents wouldn't worry about her being late. She remembered her father hugging her not so long ago. Her feeling then was that he could not make everything all right, that she was too old, that life was too complicated. That instinct was true and she sensed that much as she might like to now, there was no going back. She sensed that she was at an important place, a divergence of paths in her life. Whatever she did would settle the course of her future, the sort of person she would be. If her parents' love was like a beacon to her, it was one at a harbour mouth which she had left. She must continue on her journey without it.

She sensed that, a week before her sixteenth birthday, she was lucky to have learnt so much about life. She had learnt that Roger's way could not be hers, that it was too narrow, it led too easily to hate for all the people it was supposed to save.

She thought of Paul. She knew he believed that he loved her, but his way could not be hers. He would limit her, lead her safely to another port, one where she could rest, unchallenged and undisturbed, in his shelter and shadow. No, that would not be her way.

She was going to find her own direction and she could see, even now as she walked through the suburbs that linked Dun Laoghaire to the city, busy with the evening traffic, her hands deep in protective coat, her school bag over her shoulder, that it was going to be hard and long. In that new sure place within her she sensed that her life was going to be one of stops and starts, hesitation, progress, regression, success, failure, mistakes, learning.

This time would pass. Maybe she would give herself up to the Gardaí. Maybe she could join a different group, one that really did care about this planet and the people on it. But all that was for later. What would matter was that she would be true to herself.

That, she believed, would be possible. She braced herself against a gust of cold night wind, watched the lights of hundreds of slow passing cars, felt the fog of her anxiety disperse as the tide of her new confidence flowed. It started as a sudden relaxation in her stomach, tense for so long, and swept through her, a flash flood of joy tearing away all in its path. She smiled, a huge involuntary smile of happiness. Sorcha stepped on the bus for the city and said aloud, 'I am going to do it.'